CINDER & THE PRINCE OF MIDNIGHT

SUSAN EE

FERAL DREAM LLC

This is a work of fiction. All of the characters, organizations and events portrayed in this novel are either products of the author's imagination or used fictitiously. Any resemblance to actual persons, living or dead, or actual events is purely coincidental.

Copyright © 2019 by Feral Dream LLC

All rights reserved. For information, contact the publisher at:

www.feraldream.com

ISBN-13: 978-0-9835970-4-9

ISBN-10: 0-9835970-4-9

Books by Susan EE

Midnight Tales novels - fairy tales, Susan EE style:

Cinder & the Prince of Midnight

Penryn & the End of Days series - world-wide bestselling series.
Post-apocalyptic adventure with angels and fallen:

Angelfall (book 1)

World After (book 2)

End of Days (book 3)

Don't miss a new story from Susan EE!

Sign up to hear about her stories at:

www. S u s a n E E .com

CHAPTER 1

*C*inder ran for her life under the full moon.

She sped through the trees, jumped over streams and climbed over rocks, all the while panting so loudly that she was afraid the entire forest would betray her. Barely out of girlhood, she had had plenty of practice running and jumping, but nothing had prepared her for this.

Behind her, she could hear the hounds baying and barking. The hooves of horses clattered behind her. The men were in no hurry, other than for the sport of it. She had seen some of their warhorses decked out in bells and gold trimming with heavily embroidered bridles. It was as if the lords were about to go on a parade through the town.

Under the moonlight, they had looked as handsome as heroes of old riding in to save the damsel in distress. When she'd first seen them gathering outside the castle walls, she'd thought they were here to stop the hunt. For a moment, she thought she and the others had been saved.

But as soon as one of them leered at her, she knew she was mistaken. These noble-looking men *were* the hunters.

She thought she could hear the screaming of a wraith

horse so close that her heart skipped a few beats. She imagined a wraith horse rearing up in the air with its flaming mane and tail. But she knew the hunters only rode ordinary horses. Wraith horses were rare and not likely to be wasted on such easy prey as chasing down girls like her.

Cinder ran up a hill and took the risk of turning to see how close they were. Below her, the dogs were crossing the stream. Only a few steps behind them, the first hunters rode out of the trees on their warhorses. They were laughing, these men of the dark realm.

She spun to run but stopped short, startled. A pair of huge eyes flashed in the moonlight ahead of her.

She jumped in fright and almost screamed before she realized that the eyes belonged to a girl. The girl looked as startled and terrified as Cinder. There was a moment of relief when each realized that the other wasn't a hunter but a hunted like herself.

They both silently looked away and ran in different directions. This was Cinder's first hunt, but she shared the sense of desperation with the other people who'd already been through this before.

The ground on the hillside was slippery with dead leaves and Cinder kept slipping. She tripped on her dress and fell, painfully landing on her knees against a fallen tree. She wanted to rip the cloth and shove it away, but it was the only protection she had against the world. She grabbed it in both hands and ran.

The hounds must have caught the other girl's scent, because their barking veered off in the direction of the other girl. Cinder couldn't help but glance back.

All she saw was a forest of shadows. The full moon streamed down in broken beams through the trees.

A horse crashed through the underbrush behind her. Cinder spun to see a horse rearing up near her.

She took two steps back and tripped. The scream of the horse was defending, but it wasn't a wraith horse, just an ordinary horse. She took courage from that.

She scrambled onto her knees and was running before she was properly on her feet.

"There you are." The rider sounded drunk. And far too close behind her.

A huge weight thunked onto her back as he landed on her. She crashed down hard on her chin and arms.

Pinned under the weight of a fully grown man, her skinny muscles were no match for him.

But she wouldn't give up. Couldn't.

He put his thick, slimy lips to her face. She turned her head enough so that he ended up licking her cheek. She turned her face and bit into his jowl.

Somewhere in the nearby trees, a girl's scream echoed through the night. Men laughed in the shadows somewhere in the distance.

Her attacker turned angry. He slapped her. Then he made a fist and pounded it down toward her face.

She jerked her head out of the way. His fist landed hard against the rock that was beneath her head. He howled in his pain and fury.

She twisted, kicked and squirmed with as much force as she could. Just as she was about to slip out from under him, he grabbed the neckline of her dress and ripped it down.

Until then, she had been terrified. But now, anger boiled up, mixing with the fear.

She groped in the dirt and grabbed the first thing she could hold. A rock, solid and round. She pounded it with all her might against the attacker's head.

He gave a surprised grunt and rolled partway off her.

On pure instinct, she hit him again with the rock.

He grunted again, and this time, he lay still. It was as if he was asleep except for the trickle of wetness from his head.

Had she killed him?

She shoved his legs off her and scrambled away on her hands and knees. She looked at the rock still in her hand. She hadn't noticed before how sharp it was. She had blindly grabbed a rock by the rounded side and hit him with the sharp edge.

There was blood on that edge.

She dropped the rock and stood on her feet. He could get up any moment and attack her again.

The hounds were barking, closer now. Had they found the other girl?

She turned and ran, leaving the man bleeding on the forest floor.

CHAPTER 2

*C*inder wandered for hours, trying to find her way out of the forest of shadows. She'd sometimes hear the hounds barking or men shouting excitedly. Sometimes, she heard screams. Horrible, wretched screams.

But she stayed hidden and kept moving, knowing that eventually, she'd find the edge of the forest. When the tree shadows finally thinned and she began to hear the lowing of livestock, she almost cried in relief.

She stumbled out of the forest, feeling like she'd just clawed her way back from the dead.

By the time Cinder limped back to her house, the sky was beginning to glow red from the sunrise. Her knees were skinned and bleeding. Her dress was in tattered ruins. Her hair was so tangled that she thought she might have to cut it off.

Cinder cried when she saw her house. Big, heaving sobs as she watched the sun rise over her once-happy home.

She stood by the haystacks, a field away from the edge of the woods. That forest used to be an enchanted place of make-believe in her earlier years. The years when her papa had kept the darkness of the rest of the kingdom away from her life.

But things had changed. The forest was now a terrifying place full of nightmares and monsters. The home she had dearly loved was dominated by a woman who sold her to the hunt for shopping money.

Cinder wanted to run away and never come back. She wanted her father back. And she wanted to be the girl she once was before she left an unconscious man bleeding in the dark forest.

Cinder sat and cried for a long time, wishing for a different life. But eventually, she came to the conclusion she always did. There was nowhere else to go. The only way out of the Kingdom of Midnight was through the forest. Only a few knew the way out, and they weren't allowed to talk about it without permission of the Dark King himself.

Even if she knew how to leave the kingdom, she had no one else to go to other than her stepmother.

When Cinder limped into the house through the kitchen door, there was fresh bread and milk on the table. That was unusual.

The scent of freshly baked bread wafted to her nose. On any other day, she would have gobbled up the treat. But today, she didn't think she could stomach it. All she wanted was to sleep for a week.

She walked like an old woman up the stairs to her tiny attic room. It was too early for anyone to be up, so she wasn't surprised that she didn't see anybody.

When she got to her room, she stopped. There was a dress on the bed. It was mended and colorless, but it would replace the one she was holding together against her chest.

Helene had known what would happen.

She knew that if Cinder survived the night, her dress would be ruined. Helene knew all the horrible things that could happen to Cinder in the forest at night with those horrible men who were supposed to be heroes on their steeds.

She would have wept some more if she hadn't been so drained. Instead, she shoved the dress to the floor and slept like the dead.

The next day was an unexpectedly easy day for Cinder. She couldn't remember Helene leaving her alone for a full day before. She saw her, of course, and she still had her usual chores to do, but her stepmother didn't speak to her and wouldn't meet her eyes.

Helene had also refused to look at Cinder yesterday when she had dropped her off at the hunt and taken a bag of coins in exchange. The woman had simply turned her back and walked away while Cinder begged her not to leave her there.

Cinder didn't know exactly what would happen, but she had heard whispers of the hunt. Everyone knew about it, even if no one talked about it in polite society. But today was different. Today, everywhere she turned, someone was talking about the hunt.

Cinder walked through the open stalls of the market, trying not to look at anyone. It was a shameful thing to be one of the people in the hunt. Even the little ones sometimes threw rocks at those survivors. And now, Cinder was one of them.

"Did you hear? A girl killed a hunter last night."

She looked up. Two merchants spoke in a normal tone of voice, which was unusual when it came to the hunt.

"I did hear. But I heard it was a wild fairy that mauled him."

The first merchant lowered his voice. "That was just a story the man's family put out to try to stem the embarrassment."

"But the body was mauled, wasn't it? I heard his arm was chewed off."

The first merchant raised his eyebrows. "Some say it was the girl." He nodded knowingly.

"The girl?" The second merchant's eyes were huge. There was a spark of excitement. He swept his eyes through the crowd in the market as if he was imagining meeting that very girl right here.

Cinder turned away before he could see the guilt in her face.

She walked over to the flower stall. Her stepmother liked fresh flowers in the house whenever she had guests over. The stall was full of bright colors that smelled of honey and summer.

Her stepsisters, who unfortunately had come with her today, were whispering about the man who had been murdered. Tammy said he had been ambushed by a gang of girls in the woods. But Darlene said it was a pack of wolfkin led by a girl. The story seemed to get bigger by the minute.

"It's about time," said Silver the flower grower.

The flower vendor had silver hair like her name, and her stall was the only one in the market that sold flowers, the rarest of commodities in the land. Some said it almost took magic to grow them in the kingdom since the Dark King took over.

"What's about time?" asked Tammy.

"That one of those girls stood up to those horrible men." Silver clipped hard with her grandmother hands. She arranged flowers beside her granddaughter, Ruby, who clipped the needle-sharp thorns off long-stemmed roses.

Anyone could sign up for the hunt. The hunters paid for "volunteers" to be hunted. Desperately poor people sometimes signed up for the money, but more often, people signed up someone else they had control over. The hunters paid more for girls, so there tended to be more of them.

"They're just disreputable girls," said Tammy. "It's their lot in life to serve."

Cinder wondered if her stepsisters knew that their mother had sold Cinder into being one of those disreputable girls.

"Yes," said Darlene. "The lords get their natural aggression out of the way with them so that they can be perfectly gentlemanly to us ladies."

"Ooh." Tammy held up an orchid. "I should like this one. It matches my dress."

"That one's not for sale," said Silver.

Tammy looked perplexed. "Why would a flower peddler not have one of her flowers for sale?"

"This one's for sale, though." Silver picked up an especially thorny rose and thrust it at Tammy. "It'll go lovely with your disposition."

Tammy raised herself to her full height and looked down her nose at Silver. "You are an obnoxious, offensive woman. I'm going to tell Mama to never give you another coin again."

She turned and huffed off. Darlene snickered as she followed her sister.

Silver sighed as she put down the thorny rose. She gave Cinder a hard look. Ruby, who was a couple of winters younger than Cinder, looked up and gave Cinder a shy smile.

"Here, child," said Silver. "You look like you could use this to brighten your day." She handed Cinder the orchid.

Cinder shook her head. "I don't have any money."

"I didn't ask for money. I told your nasty stepsister that it wasn't for sale, and it isn't. It's a gift."

Cinder took the orchid. "Thank you." Her voice trembled. "It's been a long time since someone has been kind to me."

"Quit feeling sorry for yourself. It does not become you. You are a strong girl, just as your father was a strong boy. He made something of himself from nothing. None of us had anything during the war or after. But your father, he was both clever and strong. You have his blood running through your veins. Be proud of that."

Cinder tried not to let her lips quiver over the kind words. "I miss him."

Silver sighed. "When I was your age, I was already fighting in the war with both knife and sword. You think you have it tough? I'll tell you who has it tough. That girl who killed that lord during the hunt, that's who. She was probably only a slip of a girl with no choice but to defend herself. You could learn a thing or two from her."

Silver turned and began clipping her flowers as if she was still fighting the war and the flowers were her enemy.

CHAPTER 3

The next day, her stepmother's guilt had passed and Cinder's life was full of urgent chores that garnered nothing but complaints. The days passed by as she scrubbed the stairs and beat the carpets while her stepsisters took piano and dance lessons.

Cinder did her best to forget about that night of the hunt, but it was hard with everyone gossiping about it. She had nightmares of being caught. Sometimes, her nightmares included the Dark King's men dragging her out of her house while shouting accusations of murder.

A couple of days after the hunt, the kingdom was abuzz with the news of the Dark King laughing when he found out about the nobleman who was killed by a hunted girl. He found it so amusing that he declared that he would personally participate in the next hunt.

Suddenly, the hunt that had been a sordid open secret in the land was becoming the height of fashion. The dead man's family was so incensed with the embarrassment that they put a bounty on the girl's head.

"You'd better behave and be extra good, Cinder," said

Helene as she clasped her new pearl necklace around her neck. "That bounty is worth more than ten of you. I doubt anyone would believe that a ratty little thing like you could possibly accost a nobleman, but if you try me, I may lose my patience and try to sell you to them for half their bounty."

For a heart-pounding second, Cinder thought that Helene knew the truth. But if she had sniffed the possibility of money, then Helene would never have turned back to her mirror the way that she did. Cinder put her head down and scrubbed the floor, hoping that her stepmother would move on to another topic.

"Perhaps I'll get lucky," said Helene, "and you'll be the one to injure a lord on the next hunt. One can only hope that you'll earn your keep one of these days."

Cinder stopped scrubbing and looked up at Helene.

"Next hunt?" Cinder felt haunted by the thought.

"It does happen at every full moon, you know. Mouths must be fed. And young girls need to at least try to earn their keep in this household."

"Mama," said Tammy as she flounced into the room. "My ribbons are so old and faded. Must I be embarrassed every day by the poor quality of our silks?"

Helene put her arm around the girl and walked her out into the drawing room.

"No need to get upset, dear. Being the clever woman that I am, I've discovered a new income stream for us. Tomorrow, we can go to the market. You can pick out whatever colors you like."

Cinder knelt and stared at the suds on the floor. A new income stream. The next hunt. Every full moon.

Her whole body began to tremble and she could hardly breathe.

CHAPTER 4

*C*inder normally liked market days. On those days, she was free to wander around town on her own with no chores to do for a few hours other than to buy whatever looked fresh.

But today, she had a hard time enjoying anything. The next hunt was coming. It was weeks away, but it would inevitably come just as the moon would inevitably grow fat and full.

She stumbled around, only half aware of what she was buying, when she saw the flower stall.

Cinder was drawn to the stall and the silver-haired woman who was giving a basket of flowers to a customer. Cinder politely waited until the woman was gone before talking to Silver.

"Will you help me, please?" The words barely escaped her mouth.

Silver looked at her with sharp eyes. "Help you with what, child?"

Cinder looked around to make sure no one was listening. The market was busy and everyone seemed to be preoccupied with their own business. Still, she kept her voice down to a whisper.

"I'm the girl who killed the nobleman in the woods." Tears blurred her eyes as she whispered it, and her whole body trembled.

A look of surprise came across Silver's face.

"My stepmother is going to send me on the hunt again and again. Every month on the full moon. I don't know what to do." She tried her best to keep her voice from quivering.

Silver's nostrils flared and she stood tall. "Well, blubbering about it won't help you."

Cinder blinked rapidly, feeling her eyes dry at the sting of Silver's indifferent tone. There was nothing like indifference from others to make a girl stiffen her spine and trudge on. What choice did she have?

"That's better." Silver handed her a thorny rose. "Here. Come back over here and help take the thorns off. You'll at least be out of the way of my customers then."

Cinder hesitantly walked around to the other side of the stall.

Silver handed her a knife to clip and scrape the thorns. "My granddaughter Ruby used to help me, but her father has too many chores for her now."

Silver had thick gloves on to protect her hands, while Cinder had none. But Cinder didn't complain.

It was comforting to have something to do instead of fret over what would happen in a matter of weeks. She scraped and clipped, her fingers getting prickled.

When she was done with the first rose, Silver handed her more. Cinder started to say that she had her own chores to do for her stepmother, but Silver had already turned to talk to a customer. Cinder picked up a rose and began cutting off the thorns.

Silver helped customers as they came by but didn't say

anything to Cinder during the quiet times. Cinder figured that maybe she was supposed to forget that she'd ever confessed to her. Sometimes, people were like that. They pretended that a thing never happened and everyone moved on as if in silent agreement. Perhaps this was supposed to be one of those times.

Only, Cinder wouldn't be allowed to move on as if nothing ever happened because it was about to happen again soon. Her hands began to tremble and she pricked herself even more. Blood trickled down her fingers and along the rose stems.

Silver took the rose out of Cinder's hands and handed her a pair of gloves.

"Here, use these, silly girl. Don't get blood all over my flowers. You don't want some ladyship discovering a young girl's blood on her market flowers. She may get a taste for it and come after you."

Silver wiped the stem clean of blood. Cinder looked up at her nervously. Did ladies really do that?

Ladies all seemed so proper and well mannered. But she supposed her stepmother was the same way in public. In private, though, she was practically demonic.

It was much easier to de-thorn the roses with gloves on. When Cinder was done with the roses, Silver gave her the task of separating out dried flowers into bunches for sale.

"I'm sorry, but I have to go. I have chores—"

"Yes, you do. And they are not going to get done if you're gallivanting around the market."

She shoved the dried flowers into Cinder's arms. Bit by bit, Silver gave her more tasks and showed her how to do them. They talked of nothing but flowers and the mindless tasks of dealing with them.

Cinder gradually calmed down. It soothed her to be preoccupied and every time her mind drifted to thoughts of running for her life through the dark forest, Silver gave her another task to do that took up all of Cinder until she got the hang of it.

At the end of the market day, Cinder helped Silver pack up and put everything into her wheelbarrow. A heavy mood fell on the girl as she packed the flowers up for the morning.

One more day closer to the next hunt.

Silver walked away without saying goodbye. Nor did she take her flowers with her.

"Silver, you forgot your flowers."

She turned to look at Cinder.

"What are you dawdling for?" asked Silver. "Come along and bring those flowers with you. You don't expect me to push that heavy thing all the way home, do you?"

Silver turned and walked away.

CHAPTER 5

*C*inder watched Silver walking away down the market. She had already spent all day helping Silver. She'd have a full day's chores waiting for her when she got home. But she had occasionally stayed all afternoon at the market before.

She picked up the flower cart and rolled after Silver. The woman was brusque and sometimes odd, but at least Cinder knew Silver didn't hate her the way her stepmother did.

Silver lived in a cottage surrounded by flowers at the edge of the dark forest. Her tidy cottage stood in stark contrast to the other houses in town, which were mostly water-stained and dark. Those were houses with dark windows covered by drab curtains. Hardly anyone smiled or wore bright colors. Black had been the height of fashion for as long as Cinder could remember.

The only one in town who had bright flowers all around her house was Silver. Anyone else and it would have been downright weird. Only the wealthiest had flowers. So naturally, those who were most concerned with their social status had flowers on display.

17

The only exception was Silver. She was the town's only flower grower. Without her, there would be no perfume. Without her, there would be no color at the fancy ladies' balls. Without her, there would be no bees or honey in town. So Silver was accepted, if not exactly popular.

"Leave the cart there, girl, and come inside."

Cinder looked at the darkening sky. Every year, the night fell earlier than the year before. Now, it was getting dark at three in the afternoon. She didn't like the idea of walking home alone in the dark, but that was the kind of thing they were all getting used to.

Silver's cottage was bursting with color. Flowers, both fresh and dried, were everywhere. Others had tried to raise flowers without much success. But under Silver's hands, they bloomed almost year-round. The scent was glorious and full of spring, even though it was fall.

The cottage had a large hearth with a comfortable-looking rocking chair nearby. In front of that was a large table full of flowers. Silver's home welcomed Cinder with a mixed scent of roses, honey and rich stew.

She expected Silver to pause by the hearth to kindle a fire, but instead, she lit the candles and walked into the back-room. Silver was rich enough to have a two-room cottage. Only merchants and lords had multi-room houses.

It was almost unheard of for a market vendor to live in a cottage made of petrified wood with more than one room. That was testimony to how valuable her services were.

Not sure what she was supposed to do, Cinder followed Silver into the second room. As soon as she stepped into it, she gasped.

Instead of flowers draped everywhere, there were knives, swords, spikes and all manner of soldierly things. Metal glinted from all corners. Weapons and armor were hung on every wall.

"Stop looking so shocked," said Silver. "Every woman ought to have an armory in her house."

"But...why?" Cinder gaped at the glinting knives and swords made especially for smaller frames.

"Because we live in a world with violence and hate, where too many of the stories we hear are the Dark King's propaganda. Because half the population can kill women with their bare hands. Because there is nothing to save us but us."

She ran a finger along a blade, caressing it like a lover. "Anyone who lays a hand on me will bleed out before he knows what hit him."

Cinder watched her with wide eyes. "But you're a grandmother. I've seen you with your grandchildren." She blinked, trying to make sense of it.

"What of it? You think you cannot be feminine and still be a deadly fighter? You think grandmothers and flower sellers can't kill and hunt and defend herself against other hunters?"

Cinder stood in the flower grower's armory and tried to breathe.

"You asked me to help you. I cannot save you. But I can teach you to save yourself. Understand? It will be hard work. Harder than you've ever worked. And when the time comes, you'll be completely alone with not enough training to do much other than to confuse your clumsy body."

She walked around Cinder, squeezing her arms and tapping her calves.

"And if you're lucky enough to survive the next hunt, then you shall have passed your second test. Come back to me alive, and I'll teach you how to survive the next time. And the next. And the next. Eventually, you might look forward to the hunts."

Silver stopped directly in front of Cinder. "Eventually, it might be the hunters who are afraid to go into the woods under a full moon." There was a hard glint to her eyes. "As it should be."

Cinder could hardly breathe. "You'll…you'll teach me?"

Silver looked her up and down with an assessing eye. "When the Wild Wars started, I was younger than you. Skinny and gangly, with a body that hadn't grown into itself yet. I had my head full of stories of true love and Everness."

"Everness? The kingdom of sunshine and happiness? It's hard to imagine you believing in such a fairy tale."

"It's not a fairy tale. It's our neighboring kingdom, child. The Dark King guards the way to it, and commands all to speak of it as a silly fairy tale because he fears that all his subjects will go there instead of staying in Midnight."

Cinder could only blink in surprise. She couldn't simply believe Silver over a lifetime of being told that there was no such place full of sunshine.

Silver saw her resistance and sighed. "Anyway, beliefs can kill. I believed that fairies were wee creatures full of mischief and harmless fun. And that belief certainly killed many. When the Wild Wars started, we had to call the enemy 'wild fairies' because people were dying from their belief that ordinary fairies were harmless."

She moved to take down a tiny knife. "Try this." She handed it to Cinder.

The handle was bigger than the blade, but it felt light and well balanced in her hand.

"Hold it like this." Silver adjusted the knife in Cinder's hand.

"But it's so small." The blade was no bigger than Cinder's pinky finger. "How can I fight off a horseman with this?"

"You don't fight off a horseman. Not yet. For now, you fight off a man who is so preoccupied with his own power and lust that he won't be paying any attention to you. Use his belief against him."

"I don't understand. I'm all he'll be paying attention to."

"No. Not you. He'll be preoccupied with what's in his own head and body. You are just a thing to him. An animal to be conquered and consumed. That's his belief. And it can be a fatal one, just like our belief that the fairies were harmless. That was a deadly conviction at the start of the Wild Wars. Understand? The hunters have no inkling of you as a person, with a will that is not his own."

Cinder nodded even though she wasn't sure she fully understood.

Silver turned and walked out of the armory.

"What are you waiting for?" asked Silver. "We only have a couple of weeks, and you have a world of tactics to learn."

CHAPTER 6

*E*ach morning and each night, Cinder ran over to Silver's cottage to train. She learned that her wool shoes were fine for cleaning floors but not so fine for running. Silver gave her leather shoes with thick soles that helped, but she also cautioned that a survivor needed to be self-reliant. Comfortable shoes wouldn't always be available to Cinder.

So Silver made Cinder run to the cottage in the predawn hours in her bare feet. It would toughen her feet, she said. But she allowed Cinder to run back home after the sunrise with her new shoes, which was a huge relief to Cinder.

During the day, she would squeeze in all her chores at her stepmother's house as fast as she could. There was a never-ending list of things to do, and her stepfamily were constantly adding to it. But none of them were awake as early as Cinder, and all of them retired long before Cinder went to bed. So no one noticed her absence in the predawn hours and after supper.

During her visits to Silver's cottage, Cinder did as many chores as training. She fetched pails of water, lifted heavy stacks of fertilizer, and had to climb trees to collect flowers that only grew on the top branches.

"Please, Silver. I only have a few weeks before the next hunt, and I can only be here for a few hours a day. Can't I train all the time I'm here? I promise I'll come and help you if I survive the first few hunts."

"Silly girl. You are training all the time you're here. And if you do what I tell you, you'll be training all the time that you're at your stepmother's house, too."

Cinder didn't argue. Silver was a strange woman, and that was all there was to it. But Cinder couldn't fathom why Silver thought pushing the flower cart and digging holes for new plants was good training. Every night, Cinder went to bed with sore muscles and slept like a rock.

But she continued because Silver would get in an hour or two of knife lessons along with grappling lessons each day. Once every few days, Silver would teach her a new move—one for fighting hand to hand and one for the knife. Cinder liked the knife moves better. It made her feel secretly powerful to have a hidden weapon, but Silver refused to let her rely on it.

"Weapons can be taken away from you and used against you. Your strength of mind and body is always yours. Learn to rely on yourself and yourself alone. Everything else is gift, and it's a gift just for that moment."

Each night as she ran back to her stepmother's house, Cinder watched the moon grow fuller. Each night, the terror abated the tiniest bit, only to resurface in the morning with her aching body and the knowledge that she was only a girl in a kingdom full of hunters.

One night, while she ran home, three teenage boys on horses raced down the muddy road. The moon was three-quarters full, and she could see the ghostly lines of their faces.

They were handsome and clean in a way that boys seldom were. They wore leather and velvet and were laughing. The biggest one had a whip and was whipping both his horse and the other boys' horses if they got near.

The other two boys seemed undaunted by the whip and kept racing to go past the biggest boy.

Cinder moved off the road to let them pass. As they passed her, one of the younger boys raced to move past the biggest one. The older boy raised his whip and whipped it down on the younger one.

The boy cried out and fell back, dropping his rein. The horse reared up.

The boy fell backward and thudded onto the muddy road.

The oldest boy burst out laughing. The other boy didn't laugh, but neither was he jumping off his horse to see if the fallen one was all right. He put out a burst of speed to overtake the oldest boy while he was preoccupied with mocking the fallen boy.

The biggest one tried to whip the second one as he raced past him. Then the two boys sped down the road, not even looking back at the one who was lying in the mud.

"Are you all right?" asked Cinder. "Do you need help?"

"I don't need your filthy help." He lay there, curling up in the mud in his pain.

"Well, you certainly look like you need help. And if one of us is filthy, that would be you."

He tried to glare at her but was too busy trying to breathe. Then he tried to get up, trying to look dignified.

Cinder debated what to do. Should she help him? He had said he didn't want her help, so she stayed where she was.

"Good luck, then." She turned and continued to trot down the road.

"Wait." He sounded alarmed.

She stopped and turned to look at him. He was on his feet

under the three-quarter moon. He was almost as tall as her, even though they were probably about the same age.

She cocked her head at him.

"Where are you going?" he asked.

"Home. Where are you going?"

"Home as well."

"Then you'd better get going," she said. "It'll be full night before you get there at the pace you're going."

"Why are you running? Are there wild fairies about?" He looked around nervously.

"There are always wild fairies about, but I haven't seen any if that's what you're asking."

He walked toward her. "I'm headed the same direction you are."

"Would you like to run with me?"

He walked a few steps with her in silence, obviously trying not to limp. "You don't believe in walking?"

"Sure. But the longer I take to get home, the longer it'll be before I get to sleep."

She was taunting him and they both knew it. The boy was uncomfortable, maybe even afraid to be out here in the darkening night alone. It was no wonder. Cinder didn't feel safe here alone either, even though she ran this road every night.

"Let me catch my breath for a few steps, and then I'll run with you," he said. "How far is it to town?"

"Not far. Will your...friends...be there waiting for you?"

"Not likely. They're my brothers."

"Oh. I have stepsisters who behave a lot like that."

"Then we are two of a kind."

"How do you handle it?" she asked. "The anger, I mean. It's all so unfair."

He nodded. "I beat them at their own game. At least, I try to. And you?"

"I suppose I could try to do that if I knew what the game

was. But as far as I can tell, they make up the rules as they go along."

"What about your father?" he asked. "Does he set the rules?"

Cinder listened to the crunching sound of their feet as they walked along the dirt road.

"My father passed away a long time ago."

She expected him to say he was sorry to hear it, but he said no such thing.

Now, it was his turn to be quiet. The frogs and crickets filled the night and the sky was filled with stars.

"Either my brothers will kill my father, or he will kill them."

She looked over at him. He had a noble profile, with a firm jaw and straight nose. When her papa had been alive, he used to tell Cinder stories of noble men doing noble deeds. But these days, there seemed to be more and more stories of murder and mayhem from the nobility.

Silver said the kingdom had taken on a dark taint when the Wild Wars took a turn for the worse. She never said the war was lost, even though everyone knew that the last war ended when the Dark King killed the Fairy Queen and began enslaving wild fairies. It was as if for Silver, the war continued, although very slowly.

Cinder walked a little farther away from the boy, ready to defend herself if necessary. She was sure she could take him in a fair fight since he was so close to her size and age, unlike the hunters.

The boy noticed. "Don't worry. I've had enough violence for one night."

"So you won't kill me?"

"I'm not like that, not like my brothers."

"Oh."

They walked in silence for a while. They should have

been running to get home faster, but she was content to keep walking. Apparently, so was he.

"Why are you here alone at night?" he asked. "Aren't you afraid?"

"I am," she said.

"Then why?"

"I have no choice."

That seemed enough for him. Maybe like her, he was someone who was used to no choices. That made her a little sad for him.

"Do you like flowers?" she asked.

He wrinkled his nose. "Why would you ask me if I liked flowers? Do I look like a puffed-up lady who is out to catch a man?"

She frowned. "Not all ladies are like that."

"Name one."

"Well..." She didn't know any ladies other than her step-mother, who wasn't really highborn, although she liked to pretend.

"See?"

"Just because I can't name any ladies doesn't mean all of them are as you say."

"Well, I can name dozens of ladies and they're all like that."

"How sad for you."

"Why? They're mostly out to catch my oldest brother or my father's attention. They generally ignore me."

"Why?"

"I'm not important enough. Ladies like men with power and fortune."

"Sounds terrible."

"It is. But not to worry. I'll find my power and fortune one day, and then they'll all flock to me."

"Why would you want them to? You just said you didn't like them."

"So I can reject them, of course, and let them know how much I don't want them."

She gave him a sideways glance. He smiled at her, looking proud of his own humor.

Cinder rolled her eyes and shook her head. "Are you ready to run now?"

She started to trot away before he answered. It was getting late and she didn't have time to dawdle much longer.

The boy picked up his speed and kept up. He was quite an athlete, actually. Most people who dressed in fancy clothes like him barely ever walked anywhere, much less run.

She smiled a challenge at him and picked up her pace. He kept up.

She ran a little faster. He passed her.

She raced past him.

He raced past her.

Before she knew it, they were laughing. She ran as fast as she could on the sticky road, splashing mud all over herself.

Soon, they ran so fast that they didn't have enough breath to laugh. He was quite agile. They hopped over puddles, raced around stones, slipped and fell, but then got up without much fuss and raced some more.

By the time they reached the village, they were both mud-covered and out of breath.

Cinder smiled broadly at him while she huffed. He smiled back, looking equally delighted.

It was fun to race him. She couldn't remember the last time she had played with someone like that. It must have been before Papa died.

She made a face and wiped the mud caked on her leg. He did the same and then splashed her with it.

She squealed and laughed, flinging her mud back at him.

CHAPTER 7

*P*eople peered out from their shuttered windows and closed doorways. It was rare to hear laughter other than the cackling laugh of a madman. This was the high-pitched laugh of a girl and a boy, both obviously having fun.

Several people frowned, vaguely remembering times when laughing used to be a daily occurrence. Long before the Dark King took the land, long before the wars.

They saw two people who were nearly the size of adults but who behaved like children. They flung mud at each other and apparently thought that was either funny or fun. Most of the residents couldn't remember the difference between the two, and that annoyed them.

After watching them for a minute, they shuttered their windows and shut their doors, mumbling about how strange things got when the moon grew full. It was best to mind one's own business during those times, as in all times.

But there were a few people hidden amongst the many windows who secretly smiled at the sound of laughter. Laughing at night, of all things. It was like the old days when night or day, life was lived. Unlike now, when darkness brought the end of all things light.

Most of those who secretly smiled had silver in their hair and rebellion in their hearts. They remembered the way things used to be before the Wild Wars.

They wished the two young people the best and secretly promised themselves that they would be brave enough to help them should the time ever arose. And they knew it would. Trouble always came to those who laughed in public.

"What have we here?"

The boy who walked toward them was big, bigger than he had looked on his horse when Cinder first saw him on the road.

"Is that you laughing, Dante?" The second boy walked over to them.

The boy Cinder had been laughing with suddenly sobered and looked at the boys with embarrassment.

"Let's go home." The muddy boy—whose name was apparently Dante—strode off toward the bigger boys without a backward glance.

"Don't you want to take your little girlfriend?" asked the biggest boy.

"Come on, Damon," said the third boy to the bigger one. "Let's go. It's late and they might realize we're missing."

"Who won?" asked Dante as he strode toward the three horses.

"Fine, let's go." Damon turned and strode toward the horses. "I'm tired of the stench of commoners."

"Ha!" Dante clapped his hands. "Gallant won. I knew he would."

"Since when did you and Gallant band together as allies?"

"Since you started using your whip," said Gallant as he mounted his horse. He looked at Cinder then. His eyes took her in under the moonlight.

Cinder was used to being invisible. She had to admit, though, that it stung that the boy she had been laughing with only a moment ago acted as if she didn't even exist now that his brothers were here.

And this boy Gallant made her far too self-aware. He saw her. She could tell by the way he watched her. He took in the mud on her dress, her riot of curls, her running shoes made of leather that surely cost more than she could afford.

He didn't comment and didn't look particularly curious. He just saw her, which was more than the other boys or anybody else did, other than Silver.

Then he turned his horse to go, and the other two boys followed.

Dante was the last of the group to leave. He glanced back at her. It was a quick glance with some apology to it, but Cinder couldn't help but notice that he only did it when he was sure his brothers wouldn't see it. That stung too, even though it shouldn't have. Everyone knew that nobles didn't make friends with servants.

The three boys raced into the dark to wherever their estate was, and the night quickly swallowed them.

Cinder couldn't tell by their direction which house they came from. Although Cinder had lived in Midnight all her life, there were too many noble houses around the castle to know what all the nobles looked like. They often hid their faces in public behind curtained carriages and a dozen guards. Besides, she had never been one to memorize the names and faces of the hundreds of noblemen and their families the way her stepmother and sisters were always doing.

Her stepfamily lived off the dream of making good

matches for her girls, so it was part of their daily occupation to study the social hierarchy of the eligible bachelors. Cinder, on the other hand, had no such delusions. And so she simply had never cared about the nobles.

For the first time, she wished that she knew just a little about them. She would have liked to know which family those boys came from. Not that it mattered. She'd never see any of them again, of course.

Still, her curious mind churned on it. She walked the rest of the way home thinking about the boys. If Dante had been a servant like herself, would they have been friends? What had the middle boy, Gallant, seen when he looked at her? A muddy peasant who'd dared to laugh with his brother?

This whole thing was silly. Wealthy noblemen and their spawn were always causing a ruckus in town, doing whatever they felt like to whoever they felt like. She was lucky not to be running from a spontaneous hunt tonight.

Boys like them had no one and nothing to be beholden to other than their fathers and their king. And everyone knew that the king believed that fear was a good emotion to instill in his subjects.

She crawled into bed that night, too exhausted to do anything other than to halfheartedly wipe the worst of the mud off herself. The last thing she thought of before she fell asleep was what it felt like to run with Dante and laugh through the night.

CHAPTER 8

The night of the full moon came much faster than Cinder had hoped. It was the fastest month she had ever experienced, and every day felt like torture knowing that she couldn't slow the time until the hunt.

On the week of the hunt, Silver refused to let her train with her knife.

"You sound just like my granddaughter Ruby. Always impatient, always wanting to jump three steps ahead. It takes more training than you have time for to be decent with a knife. Besides, knives are a luxury that I hope you'll always have, but you can never count on that."

"So what do I fight with?"

"Weapons. Anything you can get your hands on."

"But your knife is the only one I have."

But that wasn't true, Cinder realized. She had kitchen knives that she might be able to hide in her skirt.

"Look around you. Everything you see is a weapon." Silver took off her reed sunhat and showed it to Cinder. "Even this can be a weapon. You can take the edge of the brim and slice it into your attacker's eyes."

She made a quick, brutal motion with the brim.

Cinder shut her eyes, cringing away from the hat.

"It won't debilitate someone, but it'll give you a moment's advantage. It'll put your attacker on the defensive. Understand?"

Cinder nodded.

"Whether you slice his eyes with the brim or not, he'll back up to defend himself. That's a moment when you have your opening."

She jabbed her fingers toward Cinder's throat. "He'll be defenseless against other attacks."

She kicked toward Cinder's knees and whipped her sharp elbow at her face.

Cinder backed away, but Silver never meant to hit her. She pulled back at the last second.

"Look around you," said Silver. "What else can you use to defend yourself?"

The cottage was full of flowers, utensils, bowls, clippers. Silver picked up a rose.

"Even if all you have is a flower, how can you use that to your advantage?"

Cinder took a fresh look at the flowers. "I can stab the attacker's eyes with the bottom of the stem as if it was a stick."

"Good. What else?"

"I can use the thorns."

"How?"

"I can whip the thorns against his eyes or face."

"What else?"

Cinder couldn't think of anything else. She half grinned. "I could a lie and tell him it's poisonous and that it will kill him in a horrible way."

"Exactly right. His body isn't the only thing you can attack. The hunters have the advantage not only because they are stronger and faster on their horses. They have the advantage because the girls think they've lost before they even begin."

But they have, haven't they? Cinder didn't ask this out loud. She knew better than to contradict Silver.

"Turn the conviction around. Let them believe they are superior until you're ready to surprise them. Then pound them down in both body and mind. Only a small show of force may be required to beat down your enemy. Nature does it all the time. Many animals don't get hurt beyond some scratches when they fight for a mate. It's mostly about show."

Silver raised her arms. "So be a show woman. Convince them that you are more powerful and larger than you seem. A story of a poisonous flower with deadly thorns is a great example of being larger than you are. Understand?"

Cinder nodded. "I convince them that they are weaker than me. That I somehow have power over them."

"And if you are very convincing and very lucky, you might survive the night this full moon."

Cinder swallowed. It was far easier to think of all this training as fun. But the days were speeding by and soon, one of these techniques would have to save her life.

"I'd feel better if I had a knife," she said. "A fast-acting poisoned knife."

Silver shook her head. "Poison should be used only in desperate times."

"This is a desperate time."

"A hunter would kill you before the poison killed him. Better to rely on yourself."

Silver led her outside. "Find as many things as you can that will help you in a fight. But don't move your feet. You must be rooted to your place and can only grab things that are within reach without lifting your feet."

Silver stepped back and watched.

Cinder stood in the middle of the yard. There was nothing but dirt and grass within reach.

"There isn't even a rock, Silver. What am I to do?"

"Concentrate on what is there instead of what isn't."

"I'm supposed to fight with nothing but dirt?"

"If you must. How can you use dirt?"

Cinder sighed. She wished she could spend her precious time training with the knife.

"During the time you sighed, you could have had your throat sliced by a hunter. Concentrate, girl. Or else you will not have a chance."

Cinder leaned over to grab a handful of dirt. "I could shove it in his mouth?"

"What else?"

"Smear it in his eyes?" There wasn't much conviction in her voice. The hunters would have at least a knife, while all she had to fight with was dirt.

"What else?"

"Make a mud pie and offer it to him?"

Silver bent over and picked up dirt in her hand. Without warning, she threw it at Cinder's eyes.

Cinder jumped back and shut her eyes, turning away to try to protect herself. "Stop!"

Anger bubbled up in Cinder. It was bad enough that she had to put up with her stepmother's abuse. She also had to face being a victim of the hunt. And now this?

"You could have blinded me!"

"Exactly."

Cinder blinked at Silver, wiping the dirt out of her face.

"That would have blinded you at least temporarily if I had meant for it to. Even dirt can be your ally. Now, don't move your feet and try it again. What can you reach to use as a weapon?"

This time, Cinder was in a different place and the things she could reach were a little different. There were rocks, branches, leaves with sharp needles at the edges. Then she realized that she had fabric on her body. Buttons, laces, strips of cloth that she could use to choke someone.

"That's it." Silver's eyes sparkled. "Now you're seeing it."

CHAPTER 9

*I*t was the day of the hunt.

Cinder was so scared that she could barely eat. But she ate everything she could get her hands on. It wasn't much. Just scraps from her stepfamily's table and leftover bread from the day before. But it would be enough.

She nearly gagged when her sour stomach tried to refuse the food, but she had to eat. She had to be strong tomorrow.

Her stepmother, in all her generosity, or perhaps guilt, allowed her to ignore her chores for the day. Cinder wanted to go to Silver's cottage to practice, but Silver had told her not to come that day.

She was supposed to be relaxing and gathering her mind and body for the big night. She didn't know how she was supposed to relax. She'd never felt less relaxed in her life.

So she wandered into town when she should have been trying to sleep. After all, she might not be alive tomorrow to see it.

Today was one of the major market days. Ordinarily, it was just a small collection of stalls offering local goods for everyday kitchen needs. A couple of times every moon cycle, the market swelled into a sea of stalls with merchants coming from all parts of the kingdom.

But as far as Cinder could tell, no one felt much like buying anything. Everyone was out, though, and talking about the hunt.

"Wraith horses, they say," a large woman said with much excitement in her voice. "A full herd of them."

"And a pack of wolfkin to accompany the king," said a man selling scarves.

"And the princes. They'll be going too," said another portly woman with a basket on her arm.

"What do they be expecting, I wonder?" asked an old man. "A mass of killer village girls? If they're so afraid of them, they should be recruiting the little girls to fight for the army instead of hunting them in the night."

"No one's afraid of anything, old man," said the first woman. "The Dark King would cut your tongue out for even saying so."

"It's for sport," said the fishmonger across the way. "You wouldn't understand. These nobles are daft with too much good food and wine. They got nothing to do all day but tear each other to pieces for the fun of it."

"They miss the war, they say."

"Who could miss that war?"

"The victors."

"Are you calling us commoners the losers?"

"Well, we certainly didn't win anything from the war, now, did we?" asked the fishmonger.

"The war ain't over, lad," said the old man. "Not by a long shot."

The scarf merchant sighed. It was always the older ones who proclaimed that the war wasn't over, even though the rest of the kingdom all agreed that it had been over for decades.

"Do you think it was really a girl who mauled that nobleman?"

"Doesn't matter, now, does it?" said the old man. "A girl will be found and hung for it whether it was a girl who done it or not. That's the way it always happens."

"What if it was a wild fairy?"

"There's no bounty on a fairy, you dunce. If you want the gold, it must be a girl."

"Will there be bounty hunters as well as the noblemen on the hunt tonight?"

"Aye. That's what I've heard. Bounty hunters to capture any girl who fights back. Wraith horses and a pack of wolfkin to protect the royal princes and the Dark King. It should be quite a show tonight."

Cinder had never seen a wraith horse before, but she had seen drawings of them and heard stories of what they looked like. They were said to have a flaming mane and tail. Their bodies weren't just ethereal—they were dead and reanimated. Some of them were said to be nothing but decayed corpses held together by black magic.

She knew from stories that the eyes of wraith horses could burn so hot that a person could have her own eyes burned to ashes in her sockets just by being near it.

Nobles had them, but most were kept hidden since the peasants thought them bad luck. The Dark King was said to have an entire herd of them. People said that the most powerful fairies caught by the Dark King were trapped in his wraith horses. That they'd forever be bound to him in the bodies of his wraith horses, never to be free again.

Cinder had no desire to ever see one, but she had a bad feeling that she might tonight.

"How many girls?" asked the old man.

"As many as the town can provide. They're doubling the

money paid for the girls tonight." The scarf merchant shook his head.

Cinder saw the flower stall and hesitated. Silver had told her to rest and be at peace as much as she could tonight. She knew she'd need all her energy for the hunt, but that didn't stop the jitters.

She didn't want to be caught disobeying Silver. But she hesitated a moment too soon, for Silver saw her and waved her over.

Cinder took her time getting over to the flower stall. As soon as she did, Silver gave her a bunch of thorn roses.

"Run and hide," whispered Silver as she put her hand out for coin in case anyone was watching. "You're not ready for this. It'll be a slaughter tonight."

Then Silver turned to help another customer.

Cinder stood rooted to the ground. She had felt so trapped by her stepmother that she hadn't truly considered running. Neither had it occurred to her that Silver—who seemed to miss having a good fight—would advise her to run.

There was something in the flowers. She could feel the hardness of it in the center of the bunch, hidden among the thorns.

She casually walked over to a darker, quieter part of the market and opened her bundle of flowers.

Nestled among the thorny stems was a knife smeared with what looked like black honey. Poison.

She quickly wrapped up the bundle, making sure she could easily reach the hilt if she needed it. Tonight's hunt was more than she could handle, and she and Silver both knew it.

It would be far deadlier than last month's, when the hunt had been merely a distraction for bored nobles. Tonight's hunt included royalty, which meant that it was now the height of fashion. There would be far more hunters tonight than last month. The hunters would feel free to do whatever sadistic thing they wanted and brag about it later. That was always the case when the Dark King took an interest in a sport.

And she had done her part to make it intriguing by killing a hunter. The Dark King was never interested in anything that wasn't a blood sport.

She wandered through the market, lost in her thoughts. She began to notice that she had drifted into a shadowy and quiet part of the market that she hadn't explored before.

All the customers and merchants were whispering to each other. The stalls were empty except for selections of leather collars and whips. Behind the stalls were cages. Some small, some large.

In the smaller cages, prisoners hunched down because they weren't large enough for them to stand. Some of the captives had eyes that had no whites in them. Many of them had eyes that looked like jewels glittering with blues and greens, silver and yellow.

It was hard to look at them, these crouched people. No, not people. Fairies.

They were naked and grimy. Some watched Cinder in silence. Some fluttered their wings, while others seemed to have no wings.

Cinder turned and fled back the way she had come. No matter what was back at home, this was no safer.

She could feel jeweled eyes following her as she rushed back into the main part of the market. Even the customers who were handing over bags of coins to the merchants watched her nervously, as if worried that she would call the soldiers and have them arrested for some illicit transaction.

But fairy slavery wasn't illegal by any stretch of the imagination. It was simply dangerous.

CHAPTER 10

*C*inder rushed back home, convinced that she needed to find a safe place to hide. She just needed to grab a cloak and the few coins that Silver had given her for helping her out with the flowers.

Her plan was to disappear for a couple of nights and come back after the hunt. Helene would be furious, but that was better than being hunted, wasn't it? Cinder wasn't crazy enough to think that she could survive in Midnight alone with no home and no family. That way lay certain death and worse. Fairies weren't the only ones enslaved in dark parts of the market.

She'd wished a thousand times that she could live with Silver, but Helene wouldn't allow it. Cinder would stay away from Silver tonight. She didn't want her to get in trouble because of Cinder.

She rushed into the house through the kitchen door. The kitchen should have been empty since her stepfamily almost never came into it, but today, a cage sat right in front of the door. Its door was open, and Cinder almost ran right into it as she rushed into the house.

Cinder stopped short in front of the cage. She had just enough time to think that it looked a lot like the cages that had held the fairies before someone shoved her hard from behind.

Cinder stumbled into the cage.

She spun just in time to see her stepmother slam the cage door shut.

"No!" Cinder grabbed the bars and pushed the door.

But it was too late. Helene had already locked it and was stepping away with the key.

Cinder rattled the door.

"Let me out!"

"I *am* sorry, Cinder." Helene sounded like she might actually be sorry. "I would have preferred not to do this, but you know we desperately need the money."

She sounded like she believed her own lie. The sisters entered the kitchen, one holding a jug of water and a cup, while the other held a plate with bread, cheese and slices of meat. They put down the bread and water and pushed it gingerly toward the cage with their feet.

"Enjoy," said Tammy with a smirk.

Darlene giggle behind her hand. "We're so naughty."

"It's just temporary, girls," said Helene. "Let's leave her alone in peace. She has a big night ahead. And we want her to come back safe, don't we?"

"Of course, Mamma," said Tammy. "She's like our prized horse now."

Darlene giggled again as Helene ushered her girls out of the kitchen.

"Let me out!"

Cinder called out to them until her voice broke. She finally gave up and slid to the floor. She wasn't as tall as the fairies, but there was still not enough room to stand fully upright in the cage.

She reached out for the bread and cheese. She supposed this was the feast that eased their guilt, if they had any. It all tasted like sawdust in her mouth, but she ate it anyway. She'd need her strength.

Cinder leaned against the bars of the cage, occasionally touching the knife that Silver had given her. It reassured her that she wouldn't be entirely alone and helpless out there tonight.

After a while, Cinder's muscles became stiff. She pushed herself off the floor of the cage, feeling older than her stepmother.

She had a plan. They'd have to let her out before the hunt. After all that training, Cinder felt confident that her stepfamily wouldn't be able to hold her back if she made a run for the door. They couldn't catch her once she was out of their grasp.

So she stretched and got limber as she waited for her chance to escape.

She tensed when her stepmother walked back into the kitchen. This was her chance.

But then three men came in after her. One wore the official black of a king's guard, while the other two were obviously burly laborers.

"There she is," said Helene.

The guard nodded. The two laborers walked up to Cinder's cage and began to drag it. Cinder had to sit back down and grab the bars to keep herself steady.

Helene put her hand out to the guard. He dropped a bag of coins onto her palm.

"Treat her well, and you can have her again next month," said Helene.

"No, Helene, please!"

Cinder reached out her hand to her stepmother. For a moment, Cinder thought she saw some remorse and doubt in Helene's face, but that moment passed as the men dragged Cinder out the kitchen door.

Outside, there was a cart full of cages just like hers. In each one sat a miserable-looking girl. Their ages ranged from about ten winters to fully grown women. Every one of them had the same frightened expression.

The men shoved Cinder's cage onto a ramp and pushed it into place alongside the other captives. Hers was the last cage in the cart. Around her, the younger girls sniffled and the older ones tried to soothe them.

The cart rolled slowly through town, swaying this way and that. The dust and smell of horse dung weighed the air. The girls were mostly silent, staring out into the world as though they couldn't believe what was happening. The whole town was so quiet that Cinder could hear the creaking of the wheels as it carried them closer to the forest.

Along the way, other carts joined them until there was a procession of carts full of caged girls. Some of the townspeople watched as though they couldn't stop looking, while others looked away as if they couldn't bear the sight.

They parked the carts along the fringe of the woods. Water and bread were passed along, but most of the girls had no appetite.

They all waited and watched as the sun slid down the horizon.

CHAPTER 11

*A*s dusk crept through the trees, the men let the girls out of their cages one by one. They huddled together on the far side of the line of carts, away from the woods. A chilled mist reached its tendrils out from the forest. It slithered toward the girls, who shifted away and huddled tighter.

No one, not even the guards, wanted to be anywhere near the forest on a night of a full moon. So the guards stood in a line, making sure the captives were between them and the forest.

There was no chance of anyone getting away, not with so many of the king's guards between them and the town. The commander in charge stood on a knoll, watching the guards open the cage doors.

The only place for the girls to run to was the forest itself. None of the guards seemed to be worried about the girls going into the woods before they were forced to.

Guards put out platters of food and water on a cart, along with sturdy shoes for those who had been caught barefoot. The hunters wanted a sporting hunt tonight.

Hardly anybody ate the food, but a few exchanged their worn shoes for the ones offered. One wouldn't get far running the woods without sturdy shoes.

As soon as they let Cinder out of her cage, she walked over to the food cart. It gave her a good vantage point where she could take in the situation.

Many of the girls were far too young. They didn't even have a decent chance of outrunning the hunt. The guards who corralled them looked uncomfortable doing their jobs.

A man with a grim expression placed another platter of meat on the cart beside Cinder. He looked more like a barkeep than a guard. He kept looking toward the huddling girls with sympathy.

Cinder took a chance and spoke to him.

"What would happen if I stabbed one of the guards?" she asked in a low voice.

The man paused, then picked up empty pitchers of water as though Cinder hadn't spoken.

"The other guards would be distracted," he said, not looking at her and barely moving his lips.

She took his lead and looked at the guards around the captives and pretended she wasn't having a conversation.

"Would they kill me?" she asked.

"Might do." He picked up another pitcher. "But only if they caught you. It's a full moon, and we're close enough to the forest. Laws don't apply here tonight. Not to the hunters." He lowered his voice to barely a whisper as he turned to leave. "And not to the quarry."

Cinder touched the hard knife handle in her apron pocket. The blade was poisoned. She couldn't just stab a guard in the leg and assume he'd recover.

She looked at the guards. Their commander seemed hard and unemotional, but there were guards that looked uncomfortable. She felt no guilt about stabbing one of them to free the girls, but could she kill for it?

Her foot scuffed a rock as she walked away from the food cart. It was the size of an egg with no sharp edges.

Cinder bent over and picked it up, feeling the heft of it in her hand.

Then she swung her arm back and hurled the rock at the commander.

It cuffed him in the shoulder. It couldn't have hurt much, but there was a moment of shock when he looked around in disbelief.

Cinder ran.

"Get that girl!"

She didn't turn to see if it was the commander or another guard who shouted. All she knew was that the guards who had been near her were running after her. The rest should be distracted.

She hoped that the girls could manage to sneak away. Not all of them would, but some of them might.

Cinder ran into the woods. It was the only place to go where the guards might lose her.

"She ran into the woods!" called one of the guards behind her.

"Well, go get her, you idiot! Don't just stand there."

"But commander—"

"Go!"

The sound of guards crashing through the underbrush came behind her. It was slow and reluctant. The commander must have been nearby, though, because the guards kept wading deeper into the woods.

Cinder hoped most of the guards were behind her and that the girls were taking flight. She had no trouble herself running through the underbrush, not with the panic of her fear pushing her. Even when she fell, she hardly felt it as she jumped up and kept running.

She used the noise of the guards behind her to orient herself. She knew these woods better than most. It was uncanny how quickly a person could get lost here. So she was ever so careful to only run as deep into the woods as she needed, and then to keep the sound of the guards as a compass to circle back to the edge of the woods.

By the time she felt that she'd gone far enough to risk peeking out of the forest, the gray shadows of the oncoming night were leaching out the color of the world. The moon still hadn't risen, but the air had that tension that always seemed to hang under the full moon.

Any time now, the hunt would begin.

Cinder peered around a tree at the edge of the forest. She could barely see the group of captives at the edge of the woods. The guards were tightly controlling the group, but the number of prisoners was half what it had been.

Cinder closed her eyes for a moment and wished the escapees a safe journey back home.

Home.

She opened her eyes. If the other girls had homes like hers, it wasn't worth much. But it was shelter against the night, and whoever had sold them to the guards had already been paid, so the escaped girls should be safe for another month.

Her own house had been a home once, when her father had been alive. She had laughed and played like other children. And coming home had been a happy time.

Cinder wandered along the outer edge of the darkening woods, remembering what it used to be like to have a home with someone to welcome her.

CHAPTER 12

The moon rose over the trees, full and bright. Mist hung over the forest, slithering this way and that. Cinder had always thought the full moon beautiful until now. But all it meant to her now was fear.

Her breath came out in a fog even though it didn't seem that cold yet. Soon it would be, though.

The dogs were howling already even though it was far from midnight. The wraith horses could be heard, their neighing echoing through the night, ethereal and ghostly. They didn't sound like ordinary horses any more than they looked like them.

She ran along the outskirts of the town. She had nowhere to go and no one to go to. She couldn't risk going to Silver's cottage. If she was caught harboring a runaway girl of the hunt, who knew what the Dark King would do to her. He'd skinned people alive for far less.

She had meant to run and hide, just like Silver had told her to. But instead, she was running blindly at night, under the full moon, looking for a place to hide. She might as well be part of the hunt the way things were going.

Across the field, she saw a barn. It was unusual to have animals so close to the forest, for the forest creatures were known to hunt easy prey. She guessed the barn was empty like so many farms edging the forest. Most of those had been built before the war, before the darker beasts came crawling out of the woods when the Dark King took over.

She sprinted under the moonlight across the field, feeling like a mouse running out in the open under a hawk-filled sky.

It seemed like forever before she finally reached it. She leaned against the barn door, panting. This looked like a good place to hide for the night. It was quiet and secluded.

The barn doors were padlocked, though, with a rusty old lock. She caught her breath enough to grab a rock and break open the doors.

Inside, a smoky horse with a flaming mane reared up at her. Its skin was decaying, sloughing off in places so that Cinder could catch glimpses of the slick muscles beneath its coat.

A wraith horse.

Its screams sounded tortured as its hooves pawed the air in front of her, barely missing her. Cinder backed up as fast as she could, letting the barn doors swing open.

The wraith horse nodded its head as if nodding at her. Then it galloped through the doors and out into the field.

The smoke around it shifted and floated as the horse ran into the forest.

Cinder opened her mouth to call out to it, to tell it not to go into the forest, but it was too late. She couldn't make noise and bring attention to herself, not if she wanted to live out the night.

The stories were true. Wraith horses looked as terrifying as people said. No wonder the nobles hid them from the peasants. Cinder hoped the bad-luck part of the stories weren't as true. She'd already had enough bad luck tonight.

She climbed into the barn and closed the doors. Some noble was going to be very upset when he found out that his wraith horse was gone. Why anyone would want one in the first place was beyond her. She thought it terrifying. No display of the Dark King's favor was worth that.

She climbed up to the hayloft just in case the wraith horse had a mind to come back. With all this hay in the barn, it was a miracle that the whole place didn't burn with that horse running amuck.

Cinder sat in among the hay and looked out of the open window toward the forest. She curled into a ball, wondering when they would come and find her.

Strange lights lit up the forest. Green and gold and blue. Here and gone.

Strange sounds too. Some were from the wraith horses, she knew. Others were unnatural snarling and howling. But other noises, she couldn't begin to guess. Many things were out under the moon tonight. And they were all congregating in the forest.

She sat there in the dark for a long time, expecting to not live to see the sunrise. But somehow, exhaustion overtook her and sleep crept in.

She slumped along the hay bundles, eyelids weighing heavily. Her breathing slowed, and she slipped into a deep sleep.

Cinder dreamt she was flying. Not in a contraption and not like a bird. She was like smoke and fire. In the shape of…a horse?

Her hooves pawed the air as she climbed higher above the

forest. She had no wings that she could feel. She just lifted higher by the wind the way smoke would be lifted high.

Below her, little men on their little horses raced through the woods. They were hunting. They had dogs that barked and growled, pulling on their leashes.

Then the dog keeper let his animals loose.

The dogs seemed to get larger as they leapt forward. Cinder realized they weren't dogs at all. They were more wolflike and deadlier. In her dream, they turned into a pack of wolfkin as they raced ahead, chasing prey.

A girl ran ahead of them, almost screaming in her panic. She had no chance of outrunning them and there was nowhere for her to hide.

The wolfkin were on her in an instant.

Each beast was bigger than the girl. There was a dozen of them, all pouncing on the poor thing as she fell.

After that, there was nothing but screams and growls as the writhing pack of wolfkin boiled over the girl.

The hunters came then. When they saw the wolfkin on the girl, they kept a respectful distance. They were afraid of the feeding frenzy, but they took bets on how long the screams would last. They drank wine from their leather flasks and complained about the cold beneath their furred coats.

When the wolfkin were done, they looked up with blood on their muzzles.

They looked right at Cinder, who was still floating above them with her smoky hooves and fiery mane.

The wolfkin began snarling and growling at her. Then they began to run toward her.

They leapt up, tearing at her heels. She knew they'd bite into her haunches at any moment.

She fled as fast as she could. But it was not fast enough.

The pack of wolfkin caught up and tore into her, their

faces wrinkled with their teeth bared as they ran alongside her.

Cinder was getting tired. She couldn't last much longer.

But she was angry. So angry.

The fury burned through her so fiercely that flames flared from her eyes. She had to get to the witch. A witch who could trap a fairy in the body of a rotting horse could free her as well.

Cinder kicked and bucked against the wolfkin. Several of them caught fire, but others bit and tore her haunches. She and the beasts came crashing down onto the ground.

And the pack of wolfkin leapt onto her.

CHAPTER 13

$\mathcal{C}$inder woke to the morning light hitting her face. She bolted upright, looking around at the hay bales. No one had disturbed her all night.

The hunt was over.

By the angle of the light coming in through the window, it looked like it was already past midmorning. She couldn't remember the last time she'd slept this late. Her bones and muscles ached as if she'd been running all night. The nightmares had plagued her for hours.

Outside the window, there was smoke spiraling up from the forest. The woods were always wet in the morning from the nighttime mist, so there was no worry of it all going up in flames. Still, it did not bode well.

She did her best to get the straw out of her hair and the sleep out of her eyes as she left the barn.

It was a long walk back into town. Along the way, she saw no one. It wasn't market day, so it was no surprise that the merchants weren't on the road, but townsfolk usually got up and took to the road at dawn.

The town streets had an eerie feel to them. The windows

were all shuttered and barred shut. There were no children playing, no chickens loose on the cobblestones. The town was silent except for some commotion that seemed to be happening on the far side that she couldn't see.

The few people she did see scurried about with their heads down. None of them would make eye contact with her and sped up as they passed by.

Cinder looked around, trying to figure out what was going on but could come to no conclusions. Curiosity pulled her through the windy streets of Midnight toward the sound of the commotion.

When she got to the poorest section of town, she wished she hadn't come.

The king's guards were dragging people out of the houses. They picked one or two out of each house they visited, but they seemed to randomly select the houses.

Their families cried and begged. A few attacked the guards, trying to grab their children away from them, but those parents were beaten.

One man was stabbed and left bleeding on the dirt road as the guards tossed his daughter into a cage on a cart full of caged people.

Cinder clenched her fists so hard that she dug her nails into her palm until the pain of it brought her back to herself. What was going on?

The hunt had just happened. Why were they collecting people already? And this time, it was against the wills of the families. These were not people being sold for the hunt.

She made herself turn and walk away. She could do nothing to help anyone here. Now, Cinder was like the other townspeople—silent and in shock.

Instead of heading to her stepmother's house, she found herself walking to Silver's cottage. Other than the crying and screaming in the poor section, the rest of the town was as still as a graveyard. By the time she reached Silver's cottage, she felt drained.

She knocked on the door.

Silence.

"Silver, are you there?"

Cinder knew Silver must be home since her horse and cart were still there. Her flowers were strewn everywhere as usual.

"It's me. Cinder."

More silence.

With a bad feeling in her stomach, Cinder pushed the door. It opened easily.

Inside, Silver sat in her rocking chair. She stared out the window with blank eyes.

"Silver?" Cinder approached slowly, the way she would with a wild cat. "Are you all right?"

Silver looked at her. When she recognized Cinder, her eyes shimmered with tears.

Cinder knelt by her side. "What's wrong? What's happened?"

"They took Ruby."

"Who did?" But she knew even as she asked.

"The soldiers came this morning. They went to random houses and dragged out people."

Cinder tried to take it all in but couldn't. "Why? What are they doing with them?"

"They're keeping them locked up until the next hunt, partly out of anger, I think. They also know that after last night, there would be very few who would willingly send their people out there. It's always been horrible, but at least most of the hunted came back alive. Now, the risks are too great. Only murderers and maniacs would let their families and servants be hunted in the forest now."

Cinder sat back on her haunches. "What happened last night?" Her words were barely a whisper.

Silver gave Cinder a look that was a mix of pity and anger. "The hunt went out of control and the hunters turned...savage."

Then as an afterthought, she said, "Either that, or the wild fairies are back with a vengeance."

The only ones who still worried over the Wild Wars were the elders who had lived through it. The hunters were far more of an immediate concern for Cinder.

"What do you mean the hunters turned savage?"

"The king invoked dark magic to win the war. The more he used that power, the more dependent he became on it, and the more twisted it made him. It touched all of his commanders and close noblemen. Each year, they become more rotted inside. The darkness eats away at them, demanding more, always hungry."

Cinder had heard this before. They sang of it in childhood songs to the little ones.

"The hunt was just one of the baser ways to let off steam. Everyone turned a blind eye to it because it kept the worst of the Dark King's men under control. They could play civilized if they got to let loose their darker side."

Silver hugged herself, looking like an old woman for the first time.

"What happened last night?"

"It was a slaughter."

Cinder took in a deep breath. "How many?"

Silver shook her head. "The rumors grew all morning. No one knows yet. Very few are talking about how many girls may have been killed. They're mostly talking about the hunters who were killed last night."

Silver looked at Cinder. "Was it you? Did you have

anything to do with it? They say it started with someone attacking the commander."

Fear crept up Cinder's spine. Her throwing that rock had gotten mixed up with the slaughter.

"The hunters deserved that fate," Silver said in a harsh voice. "But the girls certainly didn't. There won't be many of us left if they keep this up."

"They're going to keep them imprisoned until the next hunt?"

Silver nodded. Then she stood up with a hard look in her eyes.

"Where are they keeping Ruby?" asked Cinder.

"They took her to the castle. The captives will be under guard at all times. They will be fed and untouched until the hunt. The last thing they want is half-dead people fainting from hunger and abuse at the start of the hunt. No, they'll take care of them the way they'd take care of prized boars."

"What are we going to do?"

Silver visibly steeled herself. "We're going to train until we can't anymore. Then, when the moon is full, we're going into the forest and taking our girl back."

CHAPTER 14

*S*ilver and Cinder trained day and night. Cinder's muscles trembled at the harsh treatment. She fell into bed at night like a dead soldier and got up before dawn.

Silver began paying Cinder's stepmother with gold coins that were used before the fall of the old kingdom. Helene didn't even bother to come see Cinder or ask any questions about what she was doing at Silver's cottage. She seemed happy to trade her stepdaughter for coin.

Cinder was constantly sore and exhausted but also very grateful to Silver. They practiced climbing trees and shooting arrows from behind branches. Silver had her leaping off branches and landing on horses. They sparred with hands and feet as well as with knives.

Silver was surprisingly agile. She complained at night about her aches and pains and how she was too old for this kind of nonsense. But Cinder could see how her eyes sparked with fierce determination and maybe even enjoyment when she jabbed with her knife and silently glided over the forest ground.

Cinder, although decades younger, felt clumsy and

awkward compared to the older woman. But Silver seemed surprised at the speed of her learning.

"You're fast." Silver nodded her approval. "And smart. That's good. It wouldn't do to have my granddaughter's rescuer be slow and dumb."

She unexpectedly whipped out her fist at Cinder.

Cinder ducked and kicked at Silver's stomach. The older woman simply moved like a willow in the wind and let Cinder's foot kick by.

The month flew by and the full moon came quicker than Cinder thought possible. Silver kept reminding her that two months was nothing when it came to learning the infinitely complex world of soldiering. But Cinder felt so much more prepared than she had before.

On the day of the full moon, they rested, trying to build up energy for the long night ahead. But even Silver had problems resting. Neither of them could sleep, and Silver kept touching the daisies that she had said had always been her granddaughter's favorite.

The moon rose heavy and full over the misty night.

Wolfkin howled into the sky as wraith horses whinnied. Cinder never caught sight of a wraith horse, but she did see silhouettes of the wolfkin. They were a special breed of wolves that the Dark King favored. Some whispered that they were only seen on the full moon, and the rest of the time, they were human prisoners in the king's dungeons.

Villagers gathered around the hunters. Their breaths puffed around them in the frigid air. It smelled of horses and pine.

No one was pretending anymore. Everyone talked out in

the open about the hunt. This time, it would be a spectator sport as well as a participatory one.

For the first time, some of the families of the kidnapped victims were on horses as well. These were families who never would have sold their children and family members to the hunt. A few had spent their last coins to buy a horse to try to rescue their people.

The Dark King allowed anyone to participate in the hunt, but no one could ride into the forest until the official time. Everyone jostled each other, nerves zipping through the crowd.

Silver and Cinder were on foot, as were most of the villagers who were going to go into the forest. This was not without its dangers as the hunters would not limit themselves to the released captives of the hunt. Anyone on foot was fair game, and everyone going into the forest knew that.

Several of the hunters carried bows and arrows as well as swords. Many had what looked like armed guards around them. Cinder didn't remember that from before. She wasn't sure if that was meant for their self-defense or if it was part of the newly fashionable sport.

A group of hunters laughed in front of her. They were finely dressed in gold and silver thread. One of them turned to look at the rabble of commoners behind them.

"Taking the quarry early may have been the best idea his majesty has had in years," he said. "Look at all the free sport we'll be getting as a bonus."

The others turned and looked as well. When they did, their horses moved so that Cinder could see three young men sitting at the head of the group. Well, one was more of a man, while the other two looked more like older boys still. They were unusually young to be hunters, but there was no mistaking their rich garments.

"The audacity of the commoners," said one of the hunters. "They truly imagine stealing our quarry away from us?"

"No need to fret," said another. "Perhaps they will turn out to be the true quarry. They might put up a good fight. I'm in need of one."

A few looked nervously at that comment. A fight with the masses might be more than those hunters were looking for.

Cinder's eyes kept going to the three young men in their fine velvet and leather. The biggest boy swung his whip into the air, restless and ready to start. The middle one sat as still as a stone with his back straight and his shoulders back. The youngest one shifted as if he didn't want to be there.

Then the youngest one turned and looked right at her.

Cinder stopped breathing. He'd caught her completely unprepared. Until then, she had taken comfort in the anonymity of the crowd, lost in the excitement. She and Silver were just a girl and an old woman, both wrapped in hoods and blankets so that they were shapeless and unseen. Or so she had thought.

The boy's piercing eyes pinned her where she stood. It was Dante. And the others were Damon and Gallant.

When Dante saw her, his expression turned to surprised recognition. He quickly smothered it, but not before Gallant saw it.

Gallant turned to see what Dante was looking at. He looked right at her, but she couldn't tell if he recognized her.

When Damon, the oldest boy, turned to see what his brothers were looking at, the younger ones both turned back. Dante said something to Damon and pointed into the forest. That got Damon's attention away from Cinder before his eyes found her.

She was relieved. Damon had a mean streak in him, and she didn't want to be noticed by him.

Drums began rolling and high-pitched shouts caught everyone's attention.

Halfway between the hunters and the forest, a group of people were set loose. Like all prey, they sprinted out of the dangerously open field and into the dark forest.

CHAPTER 15

*T*he hunters laughed, taking swigs of their wine flasks. They tensed on their horses and grabbed their reins in their leather gloves.

Everyone looked to the Dark King as he rode into the hunt at the last minute. His entourage was impressively grand. His guards wore the crimson and black colors of the Kingdom of Midnight. Crimson and black banners whipped in the wind all along his procession.

The king himself was hard to see since he was shielded by so many guards. Cinder could mostly see his black armor with the crimson royal sigil on his chest.

Marching ahead of him was a line of beaters whose job it was to flush the quarry to make it easier for the hunters. They were boys mostly, thin and proud to be leading the king's procession.

Cinder's heart beat to the rhythm of the drums as the beaters marched into the forest ahead of the hunters. They were giving the victims time to get ahead. Giving them false hope that they might be able to escape.

One man jumped the line and began running toward the

forest. It was the fishmonger. His two daughters had both been taken by the soldiers. He was thin and dirty in his ragged clothes as he desperately ran to rescue his girls.

The Dark King's guards raised their bows. At the king's word, they shot their bows in unison.

An arrow hit the fishmonger in the back, and he fell.

"No peasant shall go before the king," said a voice full of doom and darkness.

Then the Dark King kicked his horse and raced into the field.

All the hunters on their horses kicked their heels and followed the king. The hunt was on. The fishmonger, who had been trying to crawl out of the way, was trampled without so much as a scream.

The last skirt of the youngest girls had barely disappeared before the horses began running toward them. The few villagers with horses raced behind the nobles. Then the rest of the families ran on foot after them to try to help their people.

As soon as Cinder began running beside Silver, she knew it was a mistake to follow the Dark King's rules. They would only find trampled grounds by the time they reached the woods.

And they'd be tired. They should have hidden in the groves on the high branches and jumped down on the helpless hunter who dared to harm anyone.

But Cinder kept running beside Silver. Although she was well into her grandmother years, Silver raced as fast as anyone. She seemed to have no trouble keeping up with the youngest and strongest lads of the town.

Some had trouble long before they reached the forest. The trampled field tripped a few. They'd spend the next several days sitting with their feet propped up until their ankles healed.

Silver and Cinder ran in their blankets and hoods until they entered the forest. The moonlight streamed into the woods in ethereal beams, contrasting the shadowy trees. The woods echoed with the barking hounds and shouts of the hunters.

The forest was so large that there was no way to find one particular girl. Cinder almost gave up hope as soon as they entered the mottled shadows.

A girl screamed to her right.

Then another to her left.

Several more screamed ahead of her.

In the past, Cinder had thought that she had been deep in the woods before the hunters had caught up with her. But she saw now that she had probably only been less than a mile in when she'd killed her hunter.

The victims had no chance to get very far into the woods before they were trodden down by the horsemen. The hunters may have wanted the glory of capturing a wild fairy, but even they didn't want to go too deep into the woods.

A fight broke out ahead of her. Two hunters on horseback against two village men on foot. The villagers had been calling out a girl's name when the hunters raced at them. One whipped a villager across the shoulder as he galloped by.

Then the hunters turned and trotted back with their whips up high.

Cinder, terrified, looked to Silver to see what she should do. Silver was running off into the shadows, ignoring the beating ahead of them.

Cinder raced to keep up with Silver, but lost sight of her. She thought she caught a glimpse of Silver's braid, so she kept going even though she began to doubt that it was her.

A girl was crying. High-pitched and panicked.

Then a roar of pain. Angry and masculine.

Cinder ran toward it, unsure what she was supposed to do.

In a large fairy circle of ancient trees, a hunter loomed over a girl. Her red hair looked like blood in the moonlight.

Ruby.

Her grandmother was nowhere in sight. It was up to Cinder to rescue her. She took a deep breath and slipped her knife into her hand.

Before she could get very far, the hunter kicked at Ruby. She rolled, avoiding the blow.

Cinder took the opening and raced to jump on the hunter's back, stabbing him with her knife.

Ruby pushed herself up from the ground and came at the hunter with a rock in her hand.

The man struggled a little longer, but the two girls kept hitting him until he lay still. Cinder had no idea if he was merely injured or dead. This time, she didn't much worry about it.

Ruby was breathing hard and staring at the unconscious hunter with wide eyes.

"Let's go, Ruby. We need to get out of here." Cinder put her hand out to grab Ruby.

Ruby looked at her, and her eyes grew even wider. She screamed.

Something sharp hit Cinder's shoulder. It burned all the way down and seared deeper after the first blow.

She fell to her knees, trying to breathe.

"Two for the price of one," said a male voice. "Father will be proud of me."

The boy stood towering over Cinder with his whip. It was the oldest of the three boys, Damon.

The other two came running behind him as he raised his whip again.

"Stop," said Dante. "She's my friend."

At that, Damon did stop. He turned to look at Dante.

Ruby launched at him. Apparently, Cinder wasn't the only one Silver had been giving fighting instructions to.

Ruby clawed at his eyes and chopped at his throat with the edge of her hand.

Damon made a choking sound and bent double. There was fury and madness in his eyes.

He whipped out at the girl. Ruby sidestepped, and he missed.

He pulled out a knife and stood with whip in one hand, knife in the other.

"Damon, let them go," said Dante. There was a command in his tone that seemed to enrage Damon.

"If we're not here to catch the prey and rough them up a little, then what are we here for?" Damon stabbed down at Ruby.

Cinder took aim and threw her knife at Damon.

It struck him in the throat.

Everyone stared at Damon as his eyes grew wide with the shock of what had just happened.

CHAPTER 16

They all watched, stunned, as Damon clawed at his throat. He looked at his brothers. In his eyes, there was denial mixed with panic and madness.

Ruby rushed to Cinder's side. The girls huddled together. In that moment, Cinder glanced at the brothers.

Neither of the boys moved to help their brother. They both stood rooted to the ground, staring with disbelief at the older boy as he choked on his own blood.

Cinder grabbed Ruby's hand and ran.

They ran through the woods as fast as they could. Cinder couldn't hear much beyond her pounding heart. And she had no idea where they were going or how to get out of the forest.

From all directions, dogs barked and growled, horses whinnied, men shouted. And soon, people began screaming from various parts of the woods.

Cinder stopped and circled, not sure of how to get out. Under the moonlight, every tree looked the same.

"Let's climb up a tree and wait until morning," whispered Ruby.

"If the dogs find us, we'll be trapped up there."

So they kept running, trying to get as far away from the barking as possible.

They crossed a stream, hoping the dogs would lose their scent. But as they were wading through, a net fell on Ruby.

She fell, entangled.

Cinder ran back, trying to untangle Ruby with her hands. She wished she'd had the nerve to take back her knife from Damon's throat. It would have taken her seconds to free Ruby if she'd had that knife.

Dogs came running out of nowhere. Their teeth seemed bigger and sharper than they should be. Their bodies rippled with muscle and strength.

A hunter laughed triumphantly as he rode toward them. "Over here! I got one."

Half a dozen riders mounted the hill, looking down at them.

Ruby looked at Cinder in a panic. They both knew that they couldn't fight their way out of this one.

"Run, Cinder." Ruby looked at her through the net. "It's your only chance."

Cinder hesitated. She wanted to be brave and loyal and save Ruby. She wanted to see the proud and happy look on Silver's face when Cinder brought her granddaughter back. She wanted to know that her friends were safe.

But Cinder's body made the choice for her. She turned and ran.

She was sure the dogs would come after her, and maybe they did. But the hunters did not. Her mind kept screaming about what might be happening to Ruby, but her body refused to slow down.

Cinder climbed the hill on the other side of the stream and looked back. The hunters congregated around their catch. Ruby struggled against her net, still trying to escape.

The men laughed, and the dogs were called back to their masters.

She wanted to see what would happen to her friend, but her instincts wouldn't let her. The men would not be satisfied for long with just one catch. They were here for the hunt, and the full moon drove them mercilessly.

In the long shadows of the moonlight, the hunters' faces were covered in shifting shadows as they surrounded Ruby. One suddenly looked up toward the hill where Cinder watched. In that moment, the hunter looked less than human.

Cinder spun and ran. She kept running even over the fallen logs, through the streams and deep into the woods.

CHAPTER 17

*C*inder was lost.

The night was still heavy with the full moon low on the horizon, ready to set. Mist flowed in and out of the mossy woods. Sometimes, even the sound of running water seemed to flow in and out.

There were times when she thought she heard dogs barking, although she couldn't tell which direction they were coming from. There were times when drunken laughter sounded too close, so she would freeze, hoping the hunters wouldn't stumble onto her.

And too many times, she heard screams. Not just girl screams, but the horror-filled screams of men being torn to pieces. At least, that was what it sounded like to her.

She stumbled through the misty, moonlit forest, exhausted and thirsty. It was dangerous to drink from the streams. People often got sick from drinking unboiled water. But the sound of the water trickling over the rocks called to her with every minute. She was nearing the time when she would have no choice but to risk drinking from wild water.

"Thirsty?" asked a woman's voice.

Cinder spun, trying to see where the voice came from.

"I have sweet water for you to drink."

Cinder spun again, thinking the voice came from behind. "Where are you?"

"Nowhere. Everywhere. Behind you and in front of you."

"Show yourself." She wasn't at all sure she wanted to see this person, but it bothered her more that she couldn't.

A woman walked toward her from the mist. At first, Cinder could have sworn she was part of the mist. But that couldn't be right, could it?

"Your wish, my command."

Cinder wasn't sure if there was sarcasm in those words.

She was the most beautiful woman Cinder had ever seen. Flawless skin, with flowing hair cascading around her. Tall and willowy, with a shimmery green dress that billowed in a breeze that Cinder couldn't feel.

The back of Cinder's neck prickled in warning. But this woman couldn't be a wild fairy. Wild fairies were said to be crazed creatures who attacked as soon as they saw a person.

"Are you real?" asked Cinder, taking a step back from her, just in case.

"As real as you. Why are you here in my forest?"

"I'm trying to get out. You should be too. Are you being hunted?"

The woman arched her eyebrow. "If there was a hunt, I'd be the hunter, not the hunted."

"You're one of the hunters?" Was she a warrior like Silver?

"Usually. But I haven't been in far too long. And there are so many who deserve it. You might be good practice."

Cinder took another step back. Her instincts were screaming to run, but her mind told her that she saw nothing truly to be afraid of.

As the woman walked toward Cinder, she tilted her head. "You're that girl."

"What girl?" Cinder took another step back.

The woman paused. "The girl who set the wraith horse free."

How did she know that? Cinder hadn't told anyone.

"Don't worry. I won't hurt you. I owe you at least that much."

"Listen, whoever you are, we both need to get out of the forest."

"Why would I do that?"

Cinder was surprised by the question. Everyone knew that the forest was a dangerous place.

"It's a full moon. The woods are full of hunters. The only safe place is outside the forest."

Interest lit up the woman's ethereal face. "Hunters? Is that what I've been hearing?"

"Yes. There are lots of them. You should hide."

"I don't hide. Not anymore. From now on, my enemies are the ones to hide."

Cinder understood that this was no ordinary person. Either the woman was a trained fighter who was daft enough to not know about the hunt, or she was some form of wild fairy, one that preferred to talk rather than attack. Cinder had never heard of a wild fairy who could control herself like that, but Silver had taught her that not everything she heard around the kingdom was true.

Besides, even if this woman was a fairy, she was too magnificent to be abused in a cramped cage like the broken creatures Cinder had seen at the market.

"If you're not going to hide," said Cinder, "then you should come with me. It's not safe here."

The woman tilted her head. "You'd take me home with you? To protect me?"

"If I can. So far, my luck with rescuing people is not so

good. I'm lost, for one thing. Do you know how to get out of the woods?"

"I do. But why would you want to leave the woods?"

This woman truly was daft. "I told you. The hunters are crawling over the woods tonight. They are not good people."

"But you are."

"Yes. So are the others they're hunting."

"Then shall we stop them? It will be fun." Her voice and eyes turned cold. "It's been some time since I've had fun."

"I'm afraid the only ones having fun are the hunters." Why couldn't this woman understand?

"Oh, I understand."

Cinder felt a tingling up her spine. Did the woman just hear her thoughts?

"Yes. Let us go have some fun."

Cinder backed away. "I need to go home."

"But you have no home."

Cinder backed away. She wanted to run but didn't want to turn her back on this lady.

"Tell me which way these hunters are, and I shall tell you which way to go to leave the woods."

Cinder hesitated. If she told her how to get to the hunters, the lady might actually go there. No good could come from that. But on the other hand, maybe a woman who could float in and out of the mist could take care of herself.

So Cinder pointed to the direction of the last hunters that she'd seen. "I don't think you should seek them out, though. They're dangerous men."

"I love dangerous men." The woman smiled a hard smile. "They're a challenge."

Then she pointed forward. "This is the way out of the forest. Good journey to you."

The woman turned and walked into the mist in the direction of the hunters. Within a few steps, she faded and blended into the mist.

Cinder turned and walked in the direction that the woman had pointed. She worried a little that it might be a trick. But she was so lost that one direction was as good as another. So she kept going.

Eventually, the woods thinned and she walked out into the broader world.

In the distance, the town looked small and vulnerable. She thought about walking away from all of it. She liked the idea of a fresh life somewhere else—somewhere without evil stepmothers and hunters. But in the end, she had nowhere else to go and no idea how to get there. Even if she managed to trek through the forest and find another kingdom, she had no reason to think that the rest of the world was any better than what she had here. Silver's stories of a mythical place that basked in the sun were just that—mythical.

CHAPTER 18

*J*n the morning, rescuers had to be sent into the woods. All day long, body after body was dragged out. Most of the dead were hunters, but there were also villagers and children old enough to have been considered decent sport. Every group had casualties.

Some of the bodies were whole and seemingly asleep, with hardly a scratch on them. The only sign of their trauma was their expressions. Their faces were frozen in screams of horror.

Some of the bodies were mangled, with bits torn out of them. Their expressions were peaceful and calm, as if their last moments were full of satisfaction and contentment.

Some were locked in battles, entangled in their web of swords and knives.

The survivors all had different stories. Of how the hunters went crazy and turned beastly. Of how the children suddenly turned from helpless prey to roaring monsters. Of how the mist came and strangled many of them.

There were even a few stories of a beautiful woman who incited the hunters into fighting among themselves for the right to pursue her. When the winners chased after her, she turned into a beast and ripped them to shreds. Those were the ones with the peaceful expressions, or so the story went.

Cinder walked slowly through town, catching bits and pieces of the gossip. She got shivers down her back as the stories got stranger and stranger. Were they talking about the woman she'd met in the woods?

Cinder went back to Silver's cottage with her feet dragging. She dreaded finding the cottage empty. And even if Silver was there, she dreaded having to tell her what happened to her granddaughter.

When she got there, Silver was sitting on the porch step waiting for her. Her dress was colorless and her hair was tied back in a careless knot.

Relief flooded Cinder when she saw that her friend had survived the night. She ran and hugged her. Silver did not hug her back.

"I'm glad you're all right." Cinder sat beside her on the step.

"I am far from all right. But that is the way of war, and I'd let myself forget that."

"How did you survive?"

"By killing as many hunters as I could. That kept me alive. And you?"

Cinder swallowed. Even though her throat was dry, she told her what happened last night.

Silver listened without comment. The longer Silver's silence went, the more worried Cinder became.

When she was done, Silver said, "That woman was a fairy. You were very lucky she found better entertainment than you."

"A wild fairy? I thought they were wild animals who couldn't help but attack whenever they saw a person."

"Not at all. The nobles just want you to believe that. War propaganda to keep people fearful."

"Aren't they under control? I mean, some nobles use them as slaves."

"The king did capture several of the strong ones and bound them to his wraith horses. But the ones that are simply enslaved probably decided to let men capture them so that they could lead an easier life in captivity."

"Being a slave to the Dark King is easier than life as a wild fairy?"

They were both avoiding the big topic. Ruby's absence was like a missing tooth that Cinder's mind kept reaching for.

"The life of a wild fairy is no joke. The strong bend the weak to their will. There are no limits to what they can make someone do when he's under their control. There are stories of what fairies do to humans. Well, it's nothing compared to what they'll do to each other. So yes, for the weak ones, life as a Dark King slave is better than life in the wild to be victimized by the stronger fairies."

"So the lady I saw in the forest—she's a strong fairy?"

"Stronger than most, I'll wager. Did you see the damage she caused?"

"Some of it. So she killed the hunters?"

"She toyed with the hunters. It was their problem that they couldn't handle it." She looked at Cinder. "That's the way the fairies think of it, I think. They often don't bother to kill. That's too easy for them and not much fun at all. For them, it seems to be all about the game, whatever game they're playing. But so often, we fragile humans just can't take it."

They sat in silence for a while, listening to the bugs chatter and the bees buzz.

"Was Ruby alive when you last saw her?" Silver's voice was quiet.

"She was."

"Could she still be alive?"

"I don't know, Silver. I tried to save her, but they threw a net over her, and there were just too many of them. I'm sorry."

Silver stared at the ground. "We'll know soon enough. They'll lay out all the bodies in front of the forest. And those who survived will be returned to their families."

But Ruby was not laid out with the row of bodies in front of the forest, nor did she limp back home. She was simply not seen again. Silver trekked through the woods during the days of summer, looking for her granddaughter, but she always came back home alone.

THE PRINCE OF MIDNIGHT

~ Two Years Later ~

CHAPTER 19

*T*he king's herald stood by the town's square by the well as he unrolled a scroll.

"Hear ye, hear ye!" he yelled. "His highness, the magnificent and great Dark King, ruler of the Midnight Realms, defender of his people, champion of all against the onslaught of the wild fairies, has declared that he will announce his heir."

The crowd surrounding him murmured. The king had started with six children but had lost all but two to suspicious accidents, dark magic and suicide. The last one had died during the hunt massacre, along with dozens of others. He had been heir to the throne.

It had been a couple of winters since the death of the crowned prince, yet the king had yet to declare an heir to the throne. That had fueled all kinds of speculation about what might have truly happened to bring about the crown prince's death. Rumors of nefarious dealings abounded.

"To celebrate this occasion, his majesty, in all his wisdom and generosity, has released the two crescent moons to trail the blood moon in the sky."

A murmur of appreciation went through the crowd, for the crescent moons had been seen last night. There had been much discussion of it since they hadn't been seen since the height of the war.

The older market vendors made sour faces as if they doubted that the king had anything to do with the moons.

"In addition, a royal ball shall be held in the honor of the occasion," continued the herald. "The royal princes shall select their brides at the ball and present them to the king. His majesty will then determine which bride is more suitable. The one with the more suitable bride will be his majesty's heir."

The herald paused to let his announcement sink in before continuing.

"All of the women of the kingdom—highborn ladies as well as commoners—are invited to the ball."

The crowd broke into shocked conversation. Royal balls were only for noble families. To be able to go to one was merely a dream for even the wealthiest of merchant families.

"His majesty also hereby commands that all fairy owners must make their fairies available for rent or purchase during the time leading up to the royal ball, so that the ladies of the land may use them as they wish."

The crowd's excitement doubled. Only the king's favorite subjects could own a fairy. It was a status symbol as much as a grant of power.

Ladies tittered and gossiped. Everyone knew that fairies could make an old woman young again, at least for a night. And that was all it would take, right?

It was said that fairies could also weave the most beautiful dresses and spin sparkly pairs of dancing shoes with only the simplest of ingredients. A lock of hair or a strip of skin from a dead girl. Of course, the corpse needed to be fresh, but every good spell needed fresh ingredients.

Cinder followed behind her stepmother and stepsisters while they weaved through the throng in the central square. Speculation had been gaining speed for months, but now, people were finally exchanging coins for their bets on which one of the two princes of Midnight would become heir.

The market was alive with talk of the princes. Even Cinder's stepsister Tammy, who didn't have the slightest interest in politics, was suddenly obsessed with which prince the king would choose as heir.

"It'll be Younger Prince, I'll bet," said Darlene with a giggle.

"I think Elder Prince is far more attractive," said Tammy. She'd once caught a glimpse of the elder prince, and she took every opportunity to remind everyone about it.

The princes had true names, of course, but only the nobles were allowed to call them by those. It was said that the royal family called each other by casual, familiar names, but only those close to the royal family even knew those names. To everyone else, they were Elder Prince and Younger Prince. The titles were simpler now that there were only two left.

"It won't matter which it will be," said Helene. "They are both fine matches for any of us."

"Any of us?" asked Tammy. "Mother, you're twenty years older than the princes."

"I still have my charms. Besides, we're buying the most powerful fairy money can buy."

"With what money?" whispered Tammy, for everyone whispered when talking about money.

Thieves in Midnight didn't listen carefully enough to distinguish between a lot of money and little money. They merely listened for the sound of coins.

"We'll figure something out," said Helene. She turned and gave Cinder an assessing look.

Cinder didn't like that look.

The last time she'd seen that look, her stepmother had sold her to the hunt. With the world falling faster into darkness and everyone adjusting to the new world, Cinder had managed to stay out of harm's way for two whole years since the hunt.

She would have to lock her door from now on.

Cinder kept her head down and let her hair fall in front of her face. It was this subservient attitude that made her stepmother the least angry. Cinder used to stand proud and defiant, daring her stepmother to do what she would to her. But she soon learned that it was better to keep her defiance private. Better to let her anger smolder behind the scenes rather than let it show on her face.

Cinder shifted the baskets on her arms. They were full of potatoes and vegetables. They'd come to the market for mundane things, but now, they were heading into Slavers Row.

CHAPTER 20

*T*wo years ago, this part of the market had been small and decent people hardly ever went into it. But it had grown over the last couple of years, and as darker tastes grew, so did Slavers Row.

Someone bumped into Cinder. It looked like all the ladies were rushing to this row.

Cinder tried to face directly ahead, trying not to see the rows of cages. The most wretched beings were on display here. Old magicians who had lost their battles with their enemies. First, second and third wives who were no longer wanted by their overlord husbands.

There were also more exotic creatures on display. Werechildren who turned into various things under the light of the moon. They were usually the least wanted of all the slaves, but people were bidding on them now, calling out bets on what each child might turn into once the moon turned full.

When they came to the fairy section at the farthest end of Slavers Row, even Cinder couldn't keep from staring.

Usually, one needed the king's permission to rent or buy

a fairy. They could wield powerful magic, and only skilled slavers could control them, or so they said. But now that the king had ordered the fairy slavers to let anyone give them money to use them, the row was flooded with eager women.

Fairies could do far more than just make a woman beautiful and young, of course, but the rental agreement would make sure they were bound to only use their magic for glamour and fashion for the ball.

"Oh, what about that one, Mama?" asked Darlene, pointing to a buxom one with canny eyes.

Helene sniffed as she looked the fairy over. "Too bold for my taste."

That translated to too expensive for her purse.

"Can we just sell Cinder?" asked Tammy. "I mean, look at her. What good will she be to us without a fairy?"

"She's right, Mama," said Darlene. "We might as well trade her in for a powerful fairy. Maybe the fairy can cook and clean as well?"

Cinder began to tremble. They had joked with her before, cruelly taunting her sometimes, but never had they said anything that felt so threatening.

Being traded to a slaver could be worse than death. Worse than anything she could imagine. Slavers dealt in misery as part of their trade, and she didn't need any more of that.

"No need, sister," said Cinder. "You can have both me *and* a fairy."

Tammy put her hand on her hip. "Is that so? Then get us a fairy, you stupid cow. What are you waiting for?"

So Cinder, not having any idea what to do, took a trembling step toward the stalls. She took a deep breath and put down her baskets at her stepmother's feet.

She ignored Helen's highbrow look and walked down the slavers' stalls as if she had any idea what she was doing.

She had to try something, didn't she? Her stepfamily may

be perfectly awful to live with, but it was better than being sold to a fairy slaver. For all she knew, fairies ate girls like her for breakfast.

The fairies stood naked and tall inside their cages. Graceful and proud even in their filth and stench.

They wore muzzles made of hard leather. But even so, many of those muzzles had soft spots in the center where they were being burnt by the fairies' acid spittle. It was said they could spit up to three feet. It was said their screeching was even worse. They'd make your ears bleed if you didn't run and cover your ears.

But it was their eyes that seemed to be their most powerful weapon. They were piercing and mesmerizing with their glittery jewel color. Their eyes were supposed to be lucky, but it seemed to Cinder that they hadn't brought much luck to the fairies who'd lost their eyes. Noblemen sometimes carried fairy eyes on a chain to bring them luck.

Cinder had talked to a pickpocket at the market once who tried to sell her a fairy eye. It was soft and squishy like any other eye, but she could swear it saw her. The pickpocket claimed that he could sell it for quite a lot of money on the black market.

The lady fairies were streaked in dirt and blood. Their breasts pointed proudly through their tattered dresses, and their chains left chafing marks on their wrists.

The male fairies looked starved in a way the female fairies did not. The slavers were afraid of their strength, and so they starved the fairies to weaken them as much as possible without killing them.

But wouldn't it serve the slavers to have the fairies be healthy and as beautiful as legends said they were in the wild? Why didn't the slavers take better care of them? They were worth a fortune, weren't they?

One of the fairies turned away from the crowd as if she'd had enough of humans gawking at her. The wounds where her wings had been chopped off were still raw and bloody. She must have been newly caught, still grieving for her freedom.

"Do you have any clean ones?" asked a fat lady holding a generous purse full of coins.

"No." The slaver spat on the mud. "Can't get near them with soap and water. They think it's cursed or something. Filthy lot. I'd exterminate them all if it wasn't for the king."

Everyone knew the Dark King had a thing for enslaving fairies. It was a hobby of his, capturing wild fairies despite, or maybe because of, the dangers. He often came to royal events with scratches across his face and acid burns on his neck. Once, he showed up to a royal hunt with all his hair singed off, or so the story went.

"Pardon me," said Cinder.

The slaver ignored her.

"Excuse me, sir?"

"Move along, girl. You can't afford one of these here. Try Stan's stall over at the end of the row. He's got some mangy ones you might be able to afford."

She wondered what he considered mangy if his were in this poor a shape. She nodded and moved back into the flow of the crowd.

Toward the end of the row, where the shadows were deepest and the wind the coldest, stood a few stalls where low moans came from. Cinder's feet hesitated. She didn't want to go there in the dark. Everyone in town knew that if someone was foolish enough to go into dark places, they were on their own. No one would come looking for them if they disappeared or screamed or called for help. Certainly, her stepfamily wouldn't come to her rescue.

But they weren't going to help her no matter where she was unless Cinder helped herself. So she took a deep breath and forced herself to move forward.

CHAPTER 21

The stalls were appalling. The stench was worse than it was in the main section, and the fairies here were too sickly to stand. Some leaned listlessly against their metal cages. Others sat or lay unmoving, staring blankly into the dark, as if they had willed their inner selves to go somewhere far away.

"What can we bargain for you, my little lady?" came a raspy voice.

Cinder startled. She hadn't seen the old man hiding in the shadows. "I, um, I'd like a fairy please."

"You would, of course you would. But that will cost you more than you have."

"How do you know what I have?"

"You're here, aren't you? If you had enough to buy a proper fairy, you wouldn't be at this end of Slavers Row."

"That would mean that your fairies are cheap." Or at least cheaper, she hoped.

"Fairies are never cheap. One may think that they may be a bargain, but they are never cheap."

Cinder cleared her throat. "I need to bring home a fairy

for my stepsisters and my stepmother. Is there one that I can rent even for a few hours?"

The slaver rubbed his beard. "Well, there is one that I wouldn't normally sell." He turned to look at one of the cages. "But if you pay full price in advance, then I might let you take her for a few days."

"It needs to be a fairy with some magic. You'll not swindle me out of my stepmother's coins to palm off a supposed fairy with no magic at all."

"Oh, this one has magic, you have my word on it."

"Enough to make beautiful ball gowns and cast a youth glamour on my stepmother?"

"Certainly. She can do all that and more."

"And she's not so sickly that she'll faint on us or pass diseases into our household?"

"Certainly not."

"How much is she?" Cinder held her breath. If the price was beyond what her stepmother could pay, then Cinder could end up in one of these cages.

"How much do you have?"

"I'm not so foolish as to tell you everything I have, for you'll simply demand that of me."

"Is it enough to buy a full-priced fairy?" asked the slaver.

Cinder fidgeted. "Well, no, otherwise I wouldn't be here."

"Exactly. The price is every coin you have. That's a bargain. Everyone will tell you that."

Cinder stared at the merchant. He was right, and they both knew it. Everyone knew that fairies were expensive. They were caught by the Dark King's best hunters. Until now, only the nobles could buy or rent one.

A part of her trembled in excitement at the possibility of coming home with a fairy. Another part of her, though, questioned why this slaver was willing to let go of a fairy for whatever it was that Cinder had in her pocket.

"Let me see this fairy."

The slaver hesitated for just a moment. Then he turned and gestured to a cage that was not large enough to let a fairy stand.

In the shadows of the small cage, a fairy crouched. She wore a tattered, colorless rag. Her skin was sallow and she was skeletal. But her eyes were full of fire.

"She looks half dead." There was something about her that tickled Cinder's memory.

"It's power that you want, isn't it? Why, she has so much power that we had to half starve the thing so she wouldn't overpower us. She's just right as she is. Don't let her command your mercy. Don't let her command anything. Feed her as little as you can—just barely enough to keep her alive—and she'll do whatever you want. Food is a great bribe for a fairy that's half-starved."

Cinder didn't want any part of this slaver or his abused fairies. Everyone knew that fairies could be dangerous, but she had no idea they were so abused. The poor thing was skin and bones crammed into a too-small cage.

"All right," said Cinder. "But you must agree to deliver her. I can't carry a cage, and she doesn't look like she can walk."

The slaver grinned. It looked rather evil to Cinder.

"Deal."

Cinder nodded.

He put out his hand for her coin purse. It occurred to her that he'd never determined just how much she had. But like most people who weren't wealthy, she only carried one bag with all her coins.

She brought out her coin bag and dumped the contents onto his outstretched palm. His hand closed around the coins immediately, as if it was a reflexive movement.

"Bring her back the day after the ball. If you don't return

her for any reason—any reason at all—then you'll owe me the full price of a living fairy. The Dark King's soldiers will get involved if a fairy goes missing. And neither you nor I are equipped to deal with the Dark King's wrath."

Cinder nodded. The king's soldiers got involved whenever anything happened these days. It was a daily occurrence to have someone dragged to the town square to be humiliated and punished for some slight or another.

Cinder told him where to bring the fairy, and he agreed he'd deliver it within the hour. He tried to hide it, but he looked suspiciously relieved.

She took one last look at her new fairy.

The thing grinned at her.

The fairy was all eyes and teeth covered in a mop of limp and colorless hair. But there was something about her that nagged at Cinder again. A memory? A story?

She shook her head and walked briskly out of Slavers Row.

CHAPTER 22

*I*t wasn't until the fairy was delivered and left crouched in her cage in the kitchen that Cinder realized she'd seen her before. Beneath all that hair hanging over her face, beneath the gaunt face and the thin body, was the woman she'd met in the forest years ago.

That was when she had no idea how to fight. She had thought she did in those days because she had had two whole months of training from Silver.

But now that she was going on two years of training, she knew just how dangerous it had been for her to believe that she could fend for herself in the forest. She had gotten lucky —very lucky—when she made it out alive the first two times.

Those hunts were legendary now. They had been the beginning of the real hunts.

Now, every nobleman in all the lands came from miles around to participate. On the full moon, every inn and guesthouse was full of travelers. Not just those who wanted to experience the excitement for themselves, but singers and storytellers who wanted fresh stories to spread, the merchants who sold luxury and necessary goods to the travelers, potion makers, dressmakers and every kind of person imaginable.

The full-moon hunts were a catalyst for the growth of the town and the kingdom itself. There were rumors that even enemies of the kingdom secretly came as guests of the Dark King to hunt human prey. Lots of hunters wore masks to hide their true identity.

It used to be nothing but a group of terrified local villagers being hunted in the night, but now, they ran side by side with strangers imported from elsewhere.

It had become a spectacle. There were the monthly hunts and the annual royal hunt. For the royal hunt, the Dark King declared a prize for the hunter with the most captives.

"Captured" was the word that the king's officials used, but everyone knew it really meant captured or killed. So long as the winner could prove their numbers, it didn't matter whether their captures were dead or nearly dead.

There were only two rules to the hunts. The first was that no one could start until the full moon rose. And the second was that the hunt ended when the sun rose. Between these two times, everything was fair game.

This year, there were disturbing rumors that the Dark King would hold the ball near the big hunt. No one believed it, though. The nobles would have to quickly bounce from the princes' ball to the royal hunt, or the other way around.

Worse, since the ball was open to all females regardless of birth or social standing, the hunt was likely to have few prey running through the woods, since it was far more lucrative to have one's daughter marry a prince than to be hunted. Having the ball on the full moon would mean that the hunt would be robbed of the usual excitement.

So no one truly believed it, but the rumors wouldn't go away. The castle servants kept talking about how all the food and decorations, all the pageantry and beautiful clothes for the ball, needed to be ready by the full moon.

There was always the possibility that the Dark King had finally gone mad. Everyone suspected he was anyway, but this would just prove it. The big annual hunt was his best legacy other than his sons.

"Is that creature our fairy?" Tammy stepped into the kitchen with a flourish of her skirts.

"It's awful. Look at it." Darlene put her perfumed handkerchief to her nose.

"What does a wretched creature like that know of noble balls and dresses?" asked Tammy.

"More than you ever will," said the fairy. Her voice hissed with lack of use. "Fairies live with royal balls and dresses every day of their lives."

"Not today," said Tammy.

"Not yesterday or last week, either, by the look of you," said Darlene.

"You doubt me?" asked the fairy.

"Absolutely," said Tammy. "Cinder, you've wasted our money, as usual. You just want to make sure we're never picked by the princes. Your jealousy will be the death of you one day."

As Tammy was speaking, her plain, at-home dress grew laces all along her neckline and wrists. Her petticoats turned into the finest rose silk, and her neck and wrists sparkled with jewels.

Darlene screeched when she saw what was happening. She turned to the fairy.

"Do that for me. Why do you do that for Tammy and not for me?"

The fairy gave her a weary look.

Darlene's dress began to turn gray with all the color leaching out of it. Her hair fell out of her coif and lay limply along her shoulder. Then it began to frizz. The laces on her dress fell off, dangling halfway, and then her seams began to tear.

Darlene screeched again while Tammy laughed.

"Wonderful, fairy!" Tammy clapped her hands. "I knew you'd be perfect as soon as I laid eyes on you."

Darlene picked up a berry pie off the kitchen table and threw it at the cage.

It splashed all over the bars and oozed down to the floor. Before it fell all the way down, the fairy scooped it up and ate it out of her hands.

"You ghastly beast," said Darlene. "I'll have you strung up for this. You just wait until Mama hears of this."

"I think she's lovely," said Tammy as she admired her new bracelet.

The fairy grinned with red berries smeared along her lips and teeth. She then licked the remaining pie off the cage bars.

The girls flounced out, bickering all the way. As their voices faded, Cinder scooped up a cup of water and put it down on the floor where the fairy could reach it.

"You're that lady I met in the forest a couple of years ago."

"Am I? I've spent many years in the forest, met many creatures including people."

"You showed me how to get out of the forest."

"And in return, what did you do for me?"

Cinder hesitated. "I pointed you in the direction of the hunters."

"The hunters." The fairy grinned. Her teeth were sharp and pointed. "I remember you now, human. That was the juiciest bit of fun I'd had in a hundred years."

Cinder picked up a crust of bread left over from breakfast and split it in two.

"You've changed," said the fairy. "Taller. More of a woman now."

Cinder reached out to give half the bread to the fairy. The fairy began to reach for it, then hesitated.

"You share bread with a fairy. What do you want from me in return?"

"Nothing. My stepmother and stepsisters have eaten their breakfast, which means it's time for ours." Cinder took a bite of her piece.

"I must know the price before I accept favors."

"It's not a favor. It's breakfast."

The fairy continued to stare at her without taking the bread.

"Fine." Cinder sighed. "Tell me your name, and I will give you the bread."

The fairy's face cleared. "Ah. I have many names. But a piece of leftover bread is worth only one, I think. You may call me Snklkolehnalyn."

"I can't pronounce that."

"What will you give me in exchange for a name you can pronounce?"

Cinder sighed. "Water? How about a pitcher—no a cup— of water?"

"Two cups."

"Deal."

"You may call me Lalyn."

"That's a lovely name. You can call me Cinder."

"Sinder. As in *sin*?"

"No. As in cinder from the fireplace."

"Ah. A dark and bitter name. It suits me better than you. Shall we switch? My name in exchange for yours?"

"I would, but my stepfamily who gave me that name would call me Cinder no matter that I gave it to you."

"We could fix that. You could be me and I, you."

Cinder looked at the wretched creature hunched in the cage. It was a reminder that things could always get worse.

"No, thank you." She took another bite of her bread. "If I let you out of that cage, will you promise not to harm anyone or to cause havoc?"

The fairy thought for a moment. "How long will I be out?"

"Well, if you stick with your promise, you'll be out for as long as you are with us. Unless my stepfamily makes you go back in. But I don't think that will be likely, since they'll think you dirty and will probably want me to deal with you myself."

"Deal. No harm, no havoc."

Cinder had a prickling of unease as she unlocked the cage.

The slaver had assured her that fairies were forced to bind themselves to their owners when they were caught. During the lease, Lalyn would be bound to Cinder and couldn't harm her.

But Cinder wasn't entirely confident that the binding would work. Perhaps the slaver didn't know that he had the fairy who'd slaughtered a dozen hunters in that famous hunt that started the current fashion.

CHAPTER 23

*W*hen the cage was unlocked, Cinder stepped back.

Lalyn paused as if unable to believe that the door was open. She slowly reached forward and crawled out.

The tall fairy unfolded out of the cage, looking long and lean. Her shape had shrunk to the shape of a skeleton, her once-beautiful dress tattered and colorless, her once-vibrant hair limp and lanky.

But her eyes were the same. Full of cunning and fire.

Cinder took another step back when she saw the eyes. They were not the eyes of a broken creature. Would the fairy want to exact revenge on Cinder for all the wrong that had been done to her by others?

"I should like a taste of meat." Lalyn licked her dry lips. "And drink wine. Do you have any here, child?"

Cinder nodded.

"What would you have me do in exchange for them?"

Cinder cut a piece of pidgin pie from last night's supper and put it on a plate.

"I would like you to accept gifts of food and drink from

me for this one meal. If you agree to my bargain, you can have this pie and a glass of wine from my stepmother's stores."

The fairy hesitated. She did not look comfortable.

"That is a hard bargain you drive, child. Taking advantage of my starved state?" She nodded. "I approve. And agree. You'll never catch me agreeing to such a humbling bargain again. You can be sure I will return the insult at some time in the future."

But her voice was soft and her eyes were more for the food than for Cinder. So Cinder felt reassured enough to give Lalyn a generous amount of pie and a glass of wine.

The fairy seemed to forget about Cinder as she ate. She ate the cold pie as if it was a feast made by a famous chef. She did not gobble it up the way a normal starved person might. Instead, she savored every bite and tasted every sip of the wine.

The fairy did not thank Cinder when she was done. Instead, she picked a spot in the corner of the kitchen, curled up on the floor and fell asleep.

The floor was hard and cold, as Cinder knew all too well. So while Lalyn slept, Cinder gathered some blankets and draped it over the fairy.

Then she went upstairs to fetch the only other dress she owned. It was worn and patched, but it was clean and far better than what the fairy was wearing. The fairy's dress would need to be thrown out.

Cinder let Lalyn sleep for hours while she did her chores. While she swept and cooked, her stepsisters were trying out different dresses to get an idea of what they would like to wear. Their plan was to get a basic outfit ready for the fairy to enhance. They wanted the most outrageous dresses and jewelry of the entire ball so that they could stand out.

Helene helped her girls, but during the lulls, she was

trying on her own dresses and looking closely at her face. Everyone knew that fairies could use magic to make someone look younger.

It wouldn't be permanent, but Helene kept saying that she only needed it for one night. Cinder was sure, though, that if Lalyn could make Helene young again, she would insist on keeping the fairy no matter the cost.

When the fairy woke, she looked at the blanket that draped her and the folded dress beside her. She looked at the dress for a long time.

"I did not ask for a blanket."

"I know. It's a gift."

"Gifts are dangerous. One gift always begets another."

"No return gift necessary."

"Gifts can enslave without asking. Gifts can warp and subvert a perfectly good relationship between two creatures. What will it cost me to accept your gifts?"

Cinder took a deep breath, trying to figure out how to allow Lalyn her dignity.

"You can make my dress look new again." Cinder hadn't had a new dress since her papa died.

Lalyn nodded. She put her palms up and swept them over Cinder's dress.

From the bottom up, the dress turned into the most beautiful gown Cinder had ever seen. It shimmered with blue and flowed like butterfly wings when she moved.

Then Lalyn did the same for her own tattered gown. It turned into a graceful confection of silk and gauze so thin that it was almost not there.

A delighted gasp came from the kitchen doorway.

"That one's mine," said Tammy, pointing to Cinder's dress.

"And that one is perfect for me," said Helene, pointing to Lalyn's dress.

"What about me?" asked Darlene. "Why am I always the one who gets left out? It's just not fair!"

"Don't fret, darling," said Helene. "The fairy will make you another dress. I'm sure she can turn the dress you're wearing into whatever you want."

"And what do I get for making this dress for you?" asked Lalyn.

"Your life," said Helene. "We bought you and can do whatever we want with you. I am your master, and I've paid good coin for your service. Now, do as I say."

Instead of cowering or getting angry, Lalyn looked interested at that, as if she was finally about to have some fun.

"You're asking me for favors without immediate return payment?"

"Of course. I own you. You will do as I say."

"As you wish, madam." A small smile lit up Lalyn's face.

The fairy lifted the old dress Cinder had folded beside her on the floor and held it up. It changed into a sparkly pink confection of chiffon and pearls.

Darlene clapped and squealed. "It's perfect! Thank you, Mama. Only, could you change the ribbons to lace?" she asked her mother instead of the fairy.

"You heard her, fairy," said Helene. "Change the ribbons into lace."

Lalyn nodded. In her eyes, she looked like she was calculating, tabulating. Was she keeping track of her services?

The ribbons changed into lace. Then all three began tweaking the designs, asking for different shades of color and more jewels on the fabric. Each time, the fairy nodded solemnly, as if agreeing to a bargain.

When they were done, they demanded that Cinder and the fairy hand over their dresses. Darlene was the most pleased of the three by this time, because she was the only one who had a dress that wasn't dirty to begin with.

Cinder took her dress off and stood in the kitchen with nothing to wear but her underskirts. But the fairy was worse, because when she began to take her dress off, she didn't even have underskirts beneath it.

Dark bruises and whip welts marred Lalyn's shoulders and back. The bumps of her spine showed through her thin skin. Scratches and scars crisscrossed her body.

Cinder teared up at the sight of the poor creature while Helene gleefully took the dress. Cinder took one of the blankets off the floor and covered Lalyn with it.

"We have nothing to wear," said Cinder. She'd only had two old dresses, and they were both gone now. "May we use a couple of your old dresses?"

Helene paused in her excitement and looked at them.

"I could make you both wear potato sacks. But I'm feeling generous. Girls, give them your oldest dresses."

"Can the fairy do our hair, Mama?"

"And jewelry? And shoes?"

"Of course she can, my darlings. That's why Mama bought her for you." She turned to Cinder. "Get her dressed and have her meet us in our chambers. We want to see what else she can do."

CHAPTER 24

For the rest of that day and all the next, Cinder's stepfamily demanded much of the fairy. They each tried countless hair styles, different-colored jewels and hundreds of shoes, for they all had a competitive shoe fetish. Their only regret was that they could only wear one pair of shoes for the princes' ball.

All this preoccupation let Cinder sneak off in the afternoon to train with Silver. Silver had been heartsick ever since her granddaughter was taken. But she continued to sell her flowers at the market, and they still trained.

"Do you wish to go to the ball?" asked Silver as she whacked a long stick at Cinder.

Cinder blocked Silver with her own stick.

"That's like asking if I want a feast for dinner. There's no chance of it, so why think about it?"

She stabbed at Silver with her stick.

Silver knocked it away and jumped toward her.

"Are you so logical? Do you not dream of a prince to sweep you away from all this?"

Cinder swept to the side, barely avoiding Silver, but losing her stick in the process.

"A girl can dream a little, I suppose."

She kicked at Silver, who kicked her back. A solid hit and fast recovery by both.

"You cannot fool me, girl. I see the wishes in your face, hear the wistful sighs. You're just like every other silly girl."

Silver collected Cinder's stick and handed it to her.

"What do you dream of, Silver?"

A cold look came into Silver's eyes. "My dreams are dark secrets." Her voice had murder in it.

"You can't get her back no matter how many you kill, Silver."

"I know this far better than you will ever know." She strode into the cottage and came back out with an armful of flowers.

"I can't go to the market with you today," said Cinder. "I have to see to my fairy."

"Watch out for that one. Never trust a fairy."

"I have no trust for the fairy. I have her for one more day, then she goes back to the slaver."

"She will not want to. If there's one thing fairies hate, it's being held captive."

"She has no choice. Just like I have no choice."

"We all have choices, even if we do not realize it." Silver put her bundle of flowers in her cart and went back for more.

Cinder helped Silver load up her cart for a special delivery to a wealthy merchant. Then she said goodbye and started her run back home.

As usual, the sun had set in the middle of the day, making people worry about whether they'd have any sun at all by next year. The road was lit only by the stars, since the moon had yet to rise.

Coming toward her on the road was a horseman. She tensed. She had no reason to fear horsemen on this or any other road. Attacks almost never happened outside of the hunt.

If two people had a problem, they could fight it out in the woods during the hunt, where there were no limits as to what could be done. No rules. No punishment.

Same was true for violent people looking for prey. They could always wait until the hunt, when they could do anything they wanted to whomever they caught, so long as their prey had signed up for the hunt. And the Dark King made sure there were plenty of incentives to ensure plenty of prey.

Silver had paid for Cinder to stay out of the hunts for as long as she could. But the Dark King raised the fees every year, tempting even moral guardians of children old enough to participate. Silver had to match that price to convince Helene not to sign Cinder up. Until one day, she couldn't anymore.

Since then, Helene had signed Cinder to the hunt each full moon.

That was when Silver let Cinder in on a secret. The grandmother warrior had been staking out a spot on the edge of the forest every hunt. She rescued whoever wandered by and guided them to safety. Sometimes, she had to get into a fight to do it, but mostly, she merely helped those who were alone. She could rescue two villagers for the energy and risk of wrestling one victim out of the clutches of hunters. So she had to do the hard math and let those villagers go.

But now that Silver couldn't keep Cinder out of the hunts, Cinder could help. So Silver showed her the place she hid during the hunt. Now, every full moon, Cinder ran straight to their hiding spot and helped rescue villagers.

They always wore masks so that nobody could recognize them.

"The more people who know a secret, the more likely it will be told," said Silver. "Good people, bad people, grateful people—it just happens."

The Dark King acquired many of the hunt's quarry through forgiveness of debt. Every year, he raised his taxes, and every year, there were more and more families who couldn't pay. Those people had a choice—go to the dungeons and work camps, or sign up a member of their family for the hunt once a month until their debts were paid in full.

Those debts could never be paid in full, though, because the king's taxes went up every year.

It was a vicious cycle that enslaved the poor into signing up either themselves or someone in their family for the hunt. The only advantage of that was that people were relatively safe the rest of the time. Most violent impulses were put off until the hunt.

So Cinder was not terribly concerned about the lone rider coming her way. But she did have a funny feeling as she watched him.

CHAPTER 25

The dark horseman trotted toward her. He blended with the night. Only the darker shadow of his form stood out against the dim glow of moonrise highlighting the hills behind him.

He wore a dark cloak and had a hood over his head, like most soldiers. Silver said it intimidated the commoners to not be able to see their faces.

He had broad shoulders and long legs. She could tell by the gold embroidery along the edge of the cloak and on the horse's bridle that this was a wealthy merchant, or possibly a noble of high birth.

What was unusual was that he was alone. Most of his ilk traveled with guards and servants.

She stepped off the road to let him pass, but he slowed down and stopped in front of her.

"Shouldn't you be preparing for the ball?" His voice was deep and masculine.

"That's for rich ladies, my lord."

"It's for every woman who wants to participate."

He pushed his hood back. He was handsome, with eyes

that looked right at her instead of through her. Usually, nobles had trouble noticing commoners.

Even in the dim light, he looked familiar.

"You look familiar," he said.

He scanned her face, her hair, her new dress. It may have been her stepsister's oldest dress, but it was the nicest dress Cinder had had since she was a young child.

"Where have I seen you before?" He cocked his head.

"I don't believe we've met, my lord."

She hated having to say "my lord." After the hunts she'd gone through, she hated all the lords.

Still, she couldn't figure out where she had seen him before either.

"Perhaps it was on market day?"

"Perhaps." He didn't sound convinced.

Behind him, another rider cantered toward them.

"What have you there, Dante?" asked the new rider. "Aren't you hogging enough women as it is?"

Dante.

Memories came flooding back. The three brothers who were now two.

The new rider must be Gallant. Now that she knew who he was, she could see traces of the boy he used to be. Both he and Dante had grown tall and handsome.

She ducked her head, hoping they wouldn't remember her. She had changed as much as they had since they last met.

"Lift your head, girl," said Dante. "I want to get a good look at you."

She lifted her eyes with only a slight tilting of her chin.

"Stubborn," said Gallant. "I like that. You haven't claimed her already, have you, Dante?"

"I don't claim beautiful women, Gallant. They come to me freely. You ought to try that sometime. I'm sure you'll find it refreshing."

"Just because you saw her first doesn't mean I wouldn't be the one to capture her."

It was a phrase that had come from the hunt. Men talked about capturing or claiming a girl. Cinder curled her hands into fists.

"She's not interested in being captured," said Dante. "Let's go." He looked back at her. "Maybe we'll see you at the ball?"

"As I've said, the ball is for wealthy ladies," Cinder replied.

"I'm not ready to go yet." Gallant looked at her more intently. "Where have I seen you before?"

Alarm tingled her spine. She could almost feel the hangman's noose slip around her neck.

She was just about to make some excuse and run when Gallant turned his horse to block Dante's view of her.

"Run along, little brother," said Gallant. "I have grownup things to do, and you're making the lady uncomfortable."

Dante shifted his horse to look around Gallant. "I know I've seen her before. It's bothering me."

"Figure it out some other time when it's not inconveniencing me. Go."

Dante took another glance at Cinder and seemed to ponder his options. He shook his head.

"No, I think I'll stay, at least until I figure out why she looks so familiar."

Gallant watched him for a moment. Cinder wondered if they were going to get into a fight. If so, that might be a good time to run.

But no such luck. Gallant turned away from his brother and looked down at Cinder.

"So the lady has a secret. What is that, I wonder?"

She felt like a rabbit in a snare. People were hanged for lesser crimes than killing the son of a nobleman.

"My brother may be a simpleton," said Gallant, "but he's not wrong here. We've both seen you somewhere, unlikely as it seems. Normally, I couldn't care less about girls I've seen, but for some reason, it's bothering me this time. Must be important."

"I sometimes sell flowers at the market."

Gallant shook his head and slipped down from his horse. He looked her over from top to bottom.

She'd grown since he last saw her. Her body had stretched and shifted, changed shape as she both grew as a woman and as a fighter.

"It's not the flowers," Gallant said. "And it's not the parties. I would have noticed you if I had seen you at a party. And if Dante had seen you first, he would have stolen you away."

"Then I'm sure I don't know where you saw me. Does it matter?"

She didn't say "my lord" and knew she could get into trouble for it, but she didn't care at the moment.

She took a step back.

He reached out and took her arm. He pulled her closer.

"Gallant, what are you doing?" asked Dante from his horse.

Gallant took a deep sniff of Cinder's hair. "I would have remembered your scent if nothing else. The scent of jasmine at midnight. You are an intriguing little thing."

Cinder's heart hammered. The last time a man had grabbed her and held her still was that first hunt in the forest.

Claustrophobia enveloped her, and she had trouble breathing. She shoved him back with so much force that he let go of her and staggered back.

Gallant looked at her in shock.

"Nice," said Dante.

She turned and ran toward the woods.

CHAPTER 26

Gallant chased her into the woods. She could hear the bushes crackling as he jumped over them right behind her.

She couldn't outrun him. He had longer legs and better shoes.

So she took her stance. She turned and punched him.

He clearly wasn't expecting it, because he leapt right into her fist.

After a moment of shock, he turned into a ball of fury. His arms sprang up for a reactionary punch and the other hand shot out to grab her.

She ducked.

But his punch never finished swinging.

Gallant struggled against Dante, who was holding back his punch.

"What are you doing?" asked Dante. "Why waste good energy on her when you could be fighting me instead?"

"Get off me!" Gallant shoved Dante back. "You only want her because I want her. You would have left her in the dirt if I hadn't shown any interest."

Gallant straightened his coat angrily. "I'm not taking anyone away from you, brother. I just think you could take your frustrations out on someone more your size."

"You can have her." Gallant sneered. "While you're wasting time on a servant girl, I'll find myself appropriate company."

He shoved Dante on his way past. Dante didn't bother retaliating.

Both Cinder and Dante let out their breaths when Gallant got on his horse and galloped off into the night.

"This is a tense time for him," said Dante. "He's not so bad usually."

Cinder's heart was still racing, and all she wanted to do was run. She didn't want to stay here and listen to Dante making excuses for his brother.

She took a step back, ready to run further into the woods.

"I wouldn't if I were you," said Dante. "It's not safe in there."

"It's not safe here, either."

"You're right. Let's walk back to the road, shall we?"

She hesitated. "You go first."

A slight smile showed on his face. "How about we go together? Side by side, like equals?"

It was unheard of for nobles to consider commoners to be equals. Maybe he mistook her for an equal because of her dress and the dim light. Or maybe he was making fun of her.

"Come on," he said. "I would feel terrible if you got carried away by a wild fairy."

She stepped beside him, relieved that she didn't have to run into the forest. "Hasn't the king caught all the wild fairies by now?"

"There's always more. My father says never to trust fairies. Playing tricks is like food and water to them."

"I'd be playing tricks too if I was treated like them."

As soon as she said the words, she regretted them. Saying anything in favor of fairies bordered on treason.

"You should be careful of what you say."

"I...I just meant that..."

"You don't need to worry about me."

"Why not?"

They were on the road now, the same road that she had walked with Dante when she first met him years ago. She still remembered that night—the night when she had laughed and flung mud on a noble boy. She hadn't felt that free since.

He walked to horse and gathered the reins. He led the horse back to her. "I'll walk you home."

"Why?"

"I'm in the mood for company."

He looked thoughtful as he watched her in the light of the rising moonlight.

"You don't need to worry about me," he said. "I haven't turned you in for what happened the last time we were together."

Cinder almost stumbled. He remembered her.

Would he arrest her now? Have her hanged for killing his brother? Hanging was probably too simple a punishment for killing a noble. There would probably be days of torture before the public hanging.

She darted a glance at the woods. Could she run faster than him? If not, could she win a fight with him?

He was taller than her now by at least a head. He had also filled out since the last time she saw him, so it wouldn't be an easy fight, should things go there.

"Don't," he said. "I'm not going to turn you in."

She wanted to believe him, but she could almost hear Silver asking if it was worth risking her life.

Cinder continued to walk with him while she thought about it, but she wanted to be out of his reach in case she needed to run. So she incrementally drifted away from him and toward the woods.

"You'll have to pardon me if I'm not willing to risk my life on your word," she said.

"Are you calling me a liar?"

Cinder's breath caught. This was a dangerous game that she was playing.

"No, of course not, my lord. I wouldn't dare insult you."

"Oh, please don't do that."

"Do what, my lord?"

He sighed. "I liked it better when you were being sincere and thinking I was a bastard nobleman. It makes me feel swashbuckling, like a pirate."

"Swashbuckling?" Cinder raised an eyebrow.

"That's exactly what I'm talking about." He pointed to her eyebrow. "Do you know when was the last time I heard someone speak freely around me?"

She clamped her mouth shut so she didn't say, "I don't care."

"The answer is never," he said. "It's surprisingly refreshing. Go on, tell me what you really think without the 'my lord' and the groveling."

"Groveling? You know the last time I saw you, you were shorter than me."

"Aha. That's what I mean. Some honesty. And you may have noticed that I'm significantly taller than you now. Bigger, too."

"Not *significantly*."

"Significantly. And don't forget bigger. Stronger, too, obviously."

"Do these things truly matter to you? Is that what the life of a noble is like? Because you might have trouble getting sympathy from the victims who are hunted by your kind on the full moon."

He sobered. "You're right. I can't compare my troubles to most people of Midnight."

"What kind of troubles does a person of your privilege have?"

"Well, I never go hungry or have to sleep out in the rain, but one political misstep can get you killed. It is nice to have a moment where I don't have to play political games or fend off other people's agendas."

"Your brother seems to be free of other people's agendas."

"Gallant has to deal with politics and live by other people's agendas as much as I do. It's why he lashes out sometimes. He's not a bad person, not really."

"Yet you don't trust him."

He sighed. "No. Even my own brother can't be trusted."

"Why not?"

"There's too much at stake."

Cinder had no idea what he was talking about. She was curious, though. Who were these boys now turned men? What had happened after she'd left them standing over their dead brother in the forest?

"You can talk to me, you know," she said. "I'm a nobody. No money, no wealthy family. No gossip will ever come from me to haunt you in your social circle."

He looked up at the starry sky where the two crescent moons were just beginning to rise.

"Do you think that night will overtake the day so that the sun never comes out?" he asked.

"I hope not. We can't live in the dark all the time. The king must know that. He'll make day and night equal again soon."

"You are naive. Do the commoners still think that the king has control over the moons and stars?"

"Sure. He released the crescent moons, didn't he?"

Dante was silent for a few steps, as if debating with himself.

"No. He didn't." His voice was quiet.

"But—"

"Those crescent moons were called by someone else, something else."

"What could have enough power to call the moons? Only the king has…" She looked at Dante with wide eyes as realization dawned on her.

Fairies.

She couldn't help but look around at the dark trees lining the road.

"Why are you telling me this?" she asked.

"I don't know. Because I can't tell anybody else. Because my brother still believes in the power of the king and can't or won't be open to the fact that the war goes on."

"What? You too? You don't look old enough to believe that."

"What do you mean?"

"Only grandparents talk about how the Wild Wars continue. It's like they can't leave the war behind."

"They're right. The fairies are just taking a break from it. A break for them could mean a few days or a century. But the night is getting longer every month, and the king is getting more and more…"

He looked around to make sure no one was listening, even though they were the only ones on the road.

"More and more what?"

"Never mind. I shouldn't have said that."

The three-quarter moon was above the horizon now. Behind it, the tips of the crescent moons peeked above the hills.

"You can talk to me," said Cinder. "I'm only a stranger. It's me who should be afraid to talk to you. You're obviously a highborn who could order my death whenever you want."

"Yet you do not fear me. You ask questions. You don't drown me in insincere flattery. You challenge me as though you were my equal."

She had a moment of fear. This was someone who was used to power, maybe more than she had thought. She took a deep breath and gathered her courage.

"It's dark," she said, "and we'll never see each other again. So what does it matter that we speak freely? Even if we did see each other again, I'll just be a servant girl, and you'll never notice me."

"Possibly, but I doubt it. You have a way of catching my attention."

They were nearing the first houses of Midnight, where enough lights flickered through windows that he would soon get a good look at Cinder's face.

It would be beyond foolish to let him see her in the light. He might not think he'd miss her in a crowd, but she was sure he would do exactly that so long as he didn't get a good look at her.

Without warning, Cinder spun and ran into the woods. It was always a place she avoided, but they were on the border of town where the forest had less power. It seemed worth the risk compared to the alternative.

When she turned to look back, Dante was standing at the edge of the town's lights, watching her run from him.

CHAPTER 27

*C*inder didn't run far. Everyone knew the woods was not a place to trifle with, even if it was close to town. If the wild fairies didn't get you, there were plenty of other creatures that would. And that was on a night without a full-moon hunt.

So she stayed along the edge of the woods and watched Dante. He stood under the light of the moon, his broad shoulders cutting a darker shadow against the night. He seemed to be looking at the place where she'd disappeared into the forest.

"Who are you?" Frost puffed out of his mouth as he spoke, lit by the moon.

The wind carried his quiet words to her ears. Cinder didn't answer and didn't move.

Dante finally turned and walked back to his horse. She watched his riding figure disappear into the distance.

Her heart raced as she ran the rest of the way back to her stepmother's house. She tried to think of everything but the two grown boys, but of course, she couldn't think of anything else.

They had both grown into fine-looking men. It was easier to think about Gallant because she didn't have mixed feelings about him. Dante was harder to think about, but he was also harder to get out of her mind.

He remembered her.

And he hadn't turned her in to be hung. Not yet. It would serve her well to remember that nobles played games that she couldn't fathom.

Look at the king, for instance. He was said to have told his sons that whichever one of his boys was careless enough to be fooled by fairy glamour didn't deserve to inherit the kingdom. That was why he allowed the captured fairies to be leased out to any woman who could afford one.

There was even a chance now that one of Cinder's step-sisters could end up being married to one of them despite being a commoner. If the fairy was powerful enough, a prince might even marry her stepmother.

Wouldn't the prince be angry about that when he found out that he'd been duped by fairy magic? This was the way the Dark King wanted one of his sons to fall so that he could choose the other as his heir. What kind of person played games like that with his own children?

Nobles and royalty, that was who.

Of course, it was also said that the Dark King never intended to die. That rumor was more believable. People said that was the root of his obsession with capturing fairies. It would take a very powerful fairy indeed to keep a person from dying, a fairy more unusual than a pure soul raised in a dark kingdom.

That night, Cinder fell asleep with the face of Dante on her mind. He had recognized her. After years of trying to forget what happened, her past was coming back to haunt her.

She dreamt of killings and hunts and full moons. Of blood flowing down her hands and not knowing whether it was hers or someone else's. She dreamt of Silver's grand-daughter, Ruby, calling out to her for help and not being able to find her in the deep, dark woods.

~

The next day, Cinder rushed downstairs before the sun rose. Exhausted and overworked as usual, she was late for training at Silver's cottage.

"Why do you stay here?" asked the fairy.

Cinder had almost forgotten about her. Lalyn was dressed in pink chiffon with too many bows. Cinder recognized it as one of Tammy's old dresses. The bottom of the dress reached barely below the fairy's knees. Her scuffed calves and ankles showed below the hem.

"Oh, you poor thing," said Cinder. "Shall we do something about that dress? We could take the bows off and maybe cut the chiffon? It's bound to rip with everyday wear."

"Why do you not murder them in their sleep?" asked Lalyn. "Or poison them with their breakfast? Stab them repeatedly with the kitchen knives?" She seemed genuinely curious.

Lalyn casually picked up a kitchen knife and ran her finger along the edge.

"You are much stronger than them with all the work that you do." Lalyn's ethereal eyes seemed mesmerized by the blade. "You run and lift heavy soup cauldrons while they lounge all day. You know how to wield a knife. I've seen you. Why do you let them be your masters when you can rule by force?"

Cinder thought about that. On her worst days, she'd had fantasies of doing evil things to her stepfamily, but she never took them seriously. She had no doubt that truly bad deeds would haunt a person for the rest of her life.

"The world is full of horrors. I don't need to add to them."

Lalyn shrugged, putting down the knife. "It's horrible for less than an hour, then the rest of your life is free of horrors. Well worth the price."

"I'm not going to murder my family."

"They're not your family. You merely live in the same house."

"They are my stepfamily." At least, that was what Helene had told Cinder when her father died. And they were the closest thing to a family she had, weren't they?

"Only in the way that servants and slaves are members of the household."

"It wasn't always this way. My father used to spoil me." Cinder smiled wistfully.

"Where is your father now?"

Her smile dried up. She didn't want to answer that. Helene had said that he married her so that Cinder wouldn't be alone when he was gone.

"Has it never occurred to you that they may have killed him for whatever reasons people use to commit such an act?"

It hadn't ever occurred to her. It wasn't like she hadn't heard of such things happening. In the Dark King's land, these things happened with alarming regularity.

But her stepmother wouldn't do such a thing. She may be a horrible bully, but she was no killer. Wouldn't Cinder know if there was a killer under her own roof?

A small voice said that her stepmother hadn't known that she lived with a killer of a nobleman. That was what Cinder was, wasn't she? A murderer. It may have been justified to save her friend, but that didn't change the fact that she'd killed someone. And she did it right in front of his brothers.

Dante's face popped into her head again. She brushed it aside, although a misty residue remained in her mind.

"Stop making mischief," said Cinder as she headed out the door. "We all have our reasons for being stuck where we are. That doesn't mean we'll be stuck here forever."

Lalyn's mouth twitched as if she was amused. She looked regal even in her hand-me-down dress as she watched Cinder leave the house.

CHAPTER 28

*C*inder and the fairy were busy for the remaining day. They cooked and cleaned, make dresses and accessories, listened to the stepsisters chatter endlessly about the upcoming ball. Much speculation was churning among the females in town about when exactly this momentous ball might happen.

"I can't believe they haven't announced the day yet," said Darlene as she tried on another necklace made by Lalyn.

"It's part of the fun," said Tammy, trying on yet another pair of shoes.

Cinder only half listened to the gossip and speculation. Half the time, she was marveling at the fashion magic that such a bedraggled fairy had. Lalyn had clearly seen many balls in her day because her fashion sense was impressive. The girls were already talking about buying her for good when they became queens and proper ladies.

The other half the time, Cinder fretted over the upcoming full-moon hunt. This was the biggest hunt of the year, and people speculated that the ball would take place either the day before or after the royal hunt. It would be just like the Dark King to pair such a bloody spectacle with the biggest romantic event of a generation.

The next morning, the date was finally announced. The princes' ball would take place on the night of the hunt.

"How can that be?" asked Tammy as she jostled her way through the market.

The whole family had come with Cinder to the market so they could hear the announcement that everyone suspected. There were even wealthy merchant ladies in the crowd today. Everyone was talking about the ball as they walked along the stalls.

"The ball will begin in the late afternoon," said a broad lady to her daughters. She was bejeweled and powdered the way a proper lady should be. She and her daughters made Cinder's stepfamily look like peasants by comparison.

"I have it on good authority that the ball will began early enough to ensure introductions and a proper supper before midnight," said the woman. "Midnight will initiate the royal hunt this year. The men will go off and do their beastly best at midnight to do whatever it is that men do in the forest on a full moon."

"But that's such a short ball, Mama," said one of her daughters. She wore a confection of soft blues and yellows. "The biggest event in my life and it'll be over in just a few hours?"

"How are we to impress the princes when we'll barely have time to be introduced to them?" asked the other daughter. She wore a matching confection of greens and silver.

"Nothing to worry about, my sweetings." The grand lady patted her daughters. "We'll make sure you're first in line to be introduced to the princes. After that, you can be sure that the ball will continue after the hunt. The men will be back, you mark my words. They always come back to their true ladies, and this will be no exception."

The girls looked worried and so did Cinder's stepsisters.

"Chin up, ladies," said the grand lady. "This is the opportunity we've all been waiting for, and we have the advantage of having the best fashion fairy in the land. Your father made sure of it."

"How do we know that's truly the case? Papa has no fashion sense whatsoever."

"Because, my dear little sweeting, your papa and I pulled some strings and acquired our fairy fresh from a hunt. The fresh ones have the most power, you know. No worn-out, dirty slave for us. Those are for tourists and amateurs."

The ladies walked slowly down the market stalls.

Cinder's stepsisters looked crestfallen.

"Is that true?" asked Darlene. "Do we have a second-rate fairy?"

"I'm so tired of having second-rate everything," said Tammy. "Why couldn't Mama marry a wealthier man?"

"Perhaps Mama will." Helene looked annoyed with her girls. Her face had fewer lines than it had only a couple of days ago. Her sagging neck was becoming firm, and her lips were fuller than Cinder had seen them in years.

"Oh, Mama," said Darlene. "Perhaps you'll find a fat merchant at the ball who will shower you with gifts."

"And who can afford to shower all of us with gifts," said Tammy, giving Cinder a sly look. She never did like Cinder's father and made sure Cinder always knew it.

"Perhaps I'll do better than that," said Helene. "Come along, girls."

Cinder knew from the fairy that Helene had greater ambitions than catching herself a fat merchant. She pressed Lalyn every moment to make her younger, more youthful in every way—her skin, her hair, her muscle tone. She was slimming down to her girlish figure. By the time the full moon rose, Helene would seem as young as her daughters.

But everyone knew that a fairy's glamour would only last a day. The only way to keep it was if the fairy recast the glamour each day. She could also improve on it if she added to the glamour before it wore off.

The old stories said that even if the greatest fairy used powerful layers of magic over a period of time, the final glamour would still only last a day unless it was recast. There were children's songs written about it from the days of old, when people and fairies exchanged commerce.

But Helene seemed to not care that the glamour was temporary. She simply had Lalyn reapply it daily. As soon as they got home from the market, Helene called the fairy into her room.

While Lalyn was applying magic layer upon layer, Cinder finished up her chores as quickly as she could. As soon as she was done, she ran over to Silver's cottage. With the ball so close, no one paid any attention to her.

She trained in the yard even though Silver was not there that day. Full moon was coming. Cinder had had years of training now, but it never felt like it was enough. Chances were decent that she could best a hunter. Her head understood that, but her heart knew that hunters ran in packs.

Silver had continued to train and protect her in the woods, but there was never a guarantee. Each month, the full moon drove Cinder to train harder.

As the moon grew fat, Cinder's fear grew with it.

CHAPTER 29

$\mathcal{C}$ inder trained hard, but she still had nervous energy when it was time to go home. She hoped her run back home through the cool night air would wind her down so she could sleep tonight. Sleep always became more precious as the full moon neared.

The background sound of the crickets and frogs accompanied her as she jogged back home under the stars.

She was halfway home when someone walked out of the shadows near the edge of the woods.

He walked onto the road before she had time to decide what to make of him.

"It's about time," said Dante as he blocked her way.

She slowed down to a walk and Dante joined her.

"What are you doing here?"

"Waiting for you. What else would I be doing out by the road at night?"

"Why?"

"Because you so rudely left in the middle of our conversation."

"It was time for me to go."

"Why did you run from me?"

"Isn't it obvious?"

"I told you I wouldn't turn you in. I'd have just as much explaining to do as you would. So would Gallant. We'd all be in trouble if we told what happened."

"You and your noble brother would be in trouble. But I'd be tortured and hung."

"No one is going to torture or hang you."

"How do you know?"

"I'll make sure of it."

She burst out laughing. "Only the king can make such promises, and I wouldn't believe him either."

"Maybe I have more power than you think."

"That's even worse. No one should ever believe it when someone in power claims he'll take care of you."

She was thinking of Helene. When she'd first convinced Cinder to call her stepmother, especially in front of other people, Helene had promised to take care of her. She'd said that she'd loved Cinder's father and couldn't imagine his little daughter fending for herself out in the world alone.

Helene had promised that she'd be the mother Cinder never knew. But she could only do that if the world believed that she had been married to Cinder's father. And Cinder had believed her. Just for a fortnight, while Helene was convincing the world that she had married Cinder's father just before he died, Cinder had believed that she wouldn't be alone.

"It sounds like you have some experience with people in power," said Dante.

"Not someone with real power in society. Just power over me."

"I'm sorry to hear that."

They walked in silence together for a time.

"Perhaps we should speak of lighter things," he said.

She scoffed. "Lighter things? In Midnight?"

He shrugged. "Life still happens here. Lighter subjects are as much part of life as darker ones."

"Do you live here or are you just visiting? Because anyone who lives here would know better."

"Oh, I know lots of things. But I feel compelled to speak the truth, and the truth is that there are lighter subjects even in Midnight."

"So what light subject do you have in mind?"

"Hmm…" He thought about it for a while, proving that lighter subjects were not so easy to think of in Midnight. "Oh, I know. How about whether or not anyone is courting you?"

She looked at him like he was daft. "Courting me?"

"Sure. You're not so terrible to look at, at least not in the dim light of night, which is where I've always seen you. For all I know, you might have crooked teeth and a lumpy nose, but I'm sure there are worse faces out there."

She glared at him. "I'll have you know that my teeth are straight and my nose is…well, not lumpy."

"Really? The next thing you'll be telling me is that you're beautiful under the starlight."

She gave him a sideways glance. "I wouldn't say such a thing."

"But others do? Do they tell you that their hearts flutter for you, my lady?"

He bowed grandly, obviously being silly.

"Do they sing poetic verses to you and tell you that they're your hero under the stars? Do they say that you should let them court you because they are rescuers of women, defenders of puppies and friends to kittens?" He waved his arms about in a dramatic gesture.

A smile snuck up on Cinder's face. "No, they don't. But you're right—they really should."

"Absolutely. Surely you must have a face that Queen would envy. One day, I shall see it in the light a for myself. Your voice, though, that I know. It's a voice t matches a songbird, and you have hair that outshines moon-light. You, my lady, deserve to be queen of the land. That's what all the lads you know should be telling you."

Cinder rolled her eyes and shook her head, but she couldn't help smiling at his flowery language.

"Which land?"

"What?" he asked.

"Which land should I be the queen of?"

"Hmm…" He tapped his chin. "'Tis true that you are far too fair to be queen of Midnight. How about Everness?"

"The land of eternal sunshine and gold? Where everyone basks in love and lives in beautiful houses and feasts happen every night?"

"That's right. No other land is worthy of such a magnificent creature as yourself."

"Are we still telling truths now?"

"Oh, absolutely. There's nothing more truthful than Everness. Who doesn't believe in sunbeams streaming down all day long and unicorns prancing about?"

"There are unicorns there?"

He shrugged. "Why not?"

"I know a truth."

"What's that?"

"You can't keep up with me."

"What?"

Cinder raced ahead on the dirt road without giving him any warning.

"Hey!" There was laughter in his voice as he ran to catch up.

Cinder was in better condition than she'd been the last time the two had run down this road. She didn't know

just that she felt free for just this

ith her with hardly any effort. He
enough to turn and taunt her by
retending to yawn.

a puddle and kicked mud at him. Then she ran. At the next puddle, he jumped in with such enthusiasm that it splashed on her.

She squealed and chased after him, threatening all kinds of harm.

By the time they reached town, they were laughing and muddy, just as they had been the first time they'd met each other.

And like that first time, years ago, people peered out from their shuttered windows and closed doorways. It was now even more rare to hear laughter. It was so rare that many of those people hadn't heard laughter since the last time these two were outside their windows.

This time, no one frowned with disapproval. This time, everyone was a little awed by it. This time, it even scared some people because it was so foreign to them.

They couldn't help but peek out and watch the couple as they flung mud at each other, laughing so hard that they seemed to have completely forgotten that they were in the kingdom of Midnight.

After watching them for a minute, a few people shuttered their windows as though afraid of what might happen if they were caught enjoying laughter, even if it was someone else's.

The young man on the street looked up with a smile at the sound of the windows closing. The ones who were watching saw the girl slip into the shadows of an alleyway while he wasn't looking.

When he turned to say something to her, she was gone.

The man looked around, but nothing moved in the shadows of the buildings.

The secret smiles of those who watched faded as they watched the man looking around, trying to find the girl. Some of them watched until he gave up. He slumped his shoulders and walked off down the street alone.

Those who watched until the end remembered why they no longer laughed themselves.

It was too hard when it ended.

CHAPTER 30

The night of the ball was the busiest that Cinder had ever seen in Midnight. The women were more preoccupied with the ball than with the full moon.

Every female in the kingdom was preparing. Ribbon prices skyrocketed, as did jewelry prices, because not everyone had managed to get a fairy with such power.

Shoes were particularly difficult, as every woman wanted to impress the princes with their shoes. Rumor had it that they liked such things.

Cinder ran herself ragged trying to do everything that her stepsisters wanted. Thankfully, Helene had locked herself up in her room for most of the day with Lalyn.

By five o'clock, the stepsisters were downstairs and ready to go. They fussed impatiently while waiting for their mother to come down. When she did, the girls gasped collectively.

Helene looked like she was in the bloom of youth. Her cheeks were rosy, her lips were full and her hair cascaded all around her in an intricate curtain of curls.

"Mama, that's not fair," said Darlene. "What if you're the

one to catch a prince tonight? That would be one less chance for me."

"Well that would be ironic," said Tammy. "The prince would be quite upset in the morning when the glamor wore off."

Stepmother's glossy lips pinched. "What makes you think I won't look like this forever?"

"Because ours is a rented fairy," said Tammy as if talking to a stupid child. "We have to return her after the ball, Mama."

Helene gave a knowing smile. "Well, we all look gorgeous for the night. There will be plenty of wealthy bachelors at the ball, and it will be the height of fashion to become engaged tonight. If the princes are doing it, then that's how the rest of nobility shall do it. So, ladies, prince or not, we might all come back with wealthy husbands."

"Oh, Mama!" Darlene's eyes sparkled as she clapped.

"You're so clever," said Tammy with admiration.

Cinder wondered if Dante would be at the ball. Helene was right. All the noble families would be there, and whatever the royal family did, the nobles copied.

It had been harder than she thought it would be to leave Dante. She didn't know if she'd ever see him again, and she didn't even say goodbye. But she had come dangerously close to standing in the light where he might get a good look at her. He might believe that he wouldn't turn her in, but she couldn't risk it.

Would Dante and his brother choose their future brides at the ball?

It didn't matter. She'd never see either of them again anyway, if she was lucky.

But no matter what she told herself, she couldn't help but feel left out. Everyone else was going. It was a once-in-a-life-time party—an invitation to walk through the front doors of the royal castle in the finest clothes she'd ever wear. For one night, it would be as if she belonged somewhere other than by the hearth, scrubbing the floor.

One day, maybe she'd meet a fine farm boy who would take her away from all this. Silver said that wishing for a boy to rescue you was a hopeless and sad occupation. Cinder secretly hoped for her own boy anyway, even if he was as poor and trapped as she was. What would it be like to have someone love her?

A memory of Dante standing in the moonlight came to her. She almost laughed. He was certainly no poor farm boy.

She sighed and got back to work. There was no point in feeling sorry for herself.

By the time the stepsisters and stepmother left the house in their overpriced carriage, Cinder was tired. She'd been so busy that she hadn't had time to be afraid of the full moon.

It's all right now, she told herself. No one had come to get her for the hunt. Safe for another month.

"Set me free, little one," said Lalyn.

The fairy's thin fingers gripped the bars of her cage. Helene had insisted that Lalyn go back to her cage when they left for the ball. She'd left strict instructions that Cinder was not to return the fairy until she said so, even though they all knew that everyone had to return their fairies to the proper owners by morning.

"You heard my stepmother. She'd kill me if I let you out. But I can get anything you want to help you be more comfortable."

"I don't mean set me free from the cage. I mean set me free."

"You know I can't do that."

Cinder absent-mindedly picked up dishes off the kitchen table. The kitchen was a mess. She hadn't had a chance to clean the breakfast dishes yet.

"You can," said Lalyn. "We fairies are bound by our own oath. When we're captured, your Dark King offers the choice of death by torture, or to bind ourselves to our owners."

"I'm not your owner. We just rented you from the slave trader."

"My oath transferred to you when that filthy slime agreed to let you have me. Until the moment you return me, I am bound to you, and only you can set me free."

Cinder put down the dishes into the sink and turned to look at Lalyn. The poor thing had gained a little weight since she first came but not much. Cinder hated the thought of making her go back to that horrible slave trader.

"You are the property of the Dark King," said Cinder sadly. "I'd be hanged if I set you free."

"Not if you're the prince's bride. You'd be part of the royal family. You could set a mere fairy free then, couldn't you?"

"But I'm not the prince's bride." Cinder picked up the broom and began sweeping. "I'm not even going to the ball."

"You could be. I could make you up and set you on your way, just like your stepsisters."

Cinder stopped sweeping and looked up at Lalyn.

"You'd be beautiful," whispered the fairy. "I saved the best for you, Cinder."

"The prince would never choose me. He wouldn't even see me. There are a hundred noble families with beautiful daughters who know which fork to use and how to property talk to a prince."

"What difference does it make? You could enjoy a fantasy night out at the ball. Your stepsisters said they'd have fire dancers and magicians, jugglers and acrobats. It's the party of a lifetime. Everyone will be there but you. So what if the princes never see you? You'll still have a magical night out. And if you do happen to catch a prince…well, setting me free would be nothing to you then."

Cinder realized she was hugging her broom tightly to her chest. She made herself relax and put the broom aside.

She had to admit, it would be fun. Just for one night. She might even catch a glimpse of Dante in all his finery.

If she disguised herself and was very careful, it was even possible that she might even get a dance with him. See him one last time.

Lalyn was right. Cinder would never get another chance to go to something like this.

CHAPTER 31

*C*inder agreed to Lalyn's deal. If she was selected to marry one of the princes, she would set the fairy free.

Lalyn smiled in pure satisfaction. She went to work immediately, transforming Cinder's old dress into the height of fashion.

The new dress was a deep violet trimmed with shimmering gold. It was the loveliest gown Cinder had ever seen. Lalyn curled her hair and piled it high on her head. Then she draped strands of pearls over them the way a princess might wear.

"I want to wear a mask," said Cinder.

"It's not a masquerade." Lalyn frowned.

"I know. Something subtle, perhaps?"

Neither Dante nor Gallant had seen her face in full light. Yet Dante had recognized her under moonlight. Besides, her stepfamily might see her.

"I won't go unless I'm at least a little hidden behind a mask."

"How will the princes be attracted to you if they can't see

your face? You must at least try to get their attention. It's part of our bargain."

"I'll try."

Cinder was confident that the princes wouldn't notice her among the hundreds of proper ladies even if she threw herself at their feet.

"But I won't go unless I have a mask. If my stepmother or sisters see me, I won't be able to get anywhere near a prince."

Lalyn sighed in a particularly human manner. Then she lifted her hands and got to work.

She made up Cinder's face with an intricate mask that sparkled with glitter on her skin. Her lips became plump and red and her cheeks glowed.

And when Cinder looked in the mirror, she couldn't believe it was her. She put her hand to touch the mask makeup on her face.

"I admit, this makes you doubly intriguing," said Lalyn. "And your stepfamily will never recognize you."

Lalyn studied the details of Cinder's dress, tightening and fluffing here and there.

"Now remember," said Lalyn, "try to attract a prince's attention as early as possible. Their papa has decreed that they only have this one night to choose a bride, so time is of the essence."

"They couldn't possibly spend quality time with everyone they meet. They'll have to pick a stranger or someone they already know."

Lalyn twitched her lips into a secret grin. "If I didn't hate the king already, I'd almost admire him for his twisted games."

The fairy fluffed one last piece of Cinder's dress. "Ready?"

Cinder nodded. A wave of nervousness washed over her.

"How will I get there? There are no carriages left in the entire kingdom."

The fairy arched her eyebrow as if she couldn't believe Cinder was doubting her. She looked at the wall and cooed.

Seven mice scampered out of the wall and out the kitchen door.

"Come along, my lady," said Lalyn. "You have a prince waiting for you."

Outside, the fairy transformed the mice into a set of six matching horses. The seventh one turned into a rather funny-looking coachman.

Cinder glanced at the fairy sideways, wondering if Lalyn understood how transportation worked outside the forest.

"You doubt," said Lalyn.

The fairy waved her arms. One of the pumpkins in the garden grew and dimpled until it turned into a pumpkin-shaped coach.

The coachman led his fellow mice-horses to the coach and attached them. He then opened the door for Cinder to enter.

When she set foot on the coach step, her old boots peeked out from beneath the glossy hem. Battered and dusty, the old leather looked terrible beneath her dress.

"We can't have that," said Lalyn. "The princes are known for appreciating a good pair of shoes." The fairy waved her hands.

"Wait. Can I carry them as my fan or something?"

Cinder had no need for her boots. But the full moon was beginning to rise on the horizon, gathering the usual tension along with it. It was an ingrained habit now to always have her leather boots with her on the rare nights that she left the house on a full moon. The thought of being without them made her feel trapped and vulnerable.

The fairy nodded.

Cinder took her shoes off, and they turned into a fan and a small ladies' dance card.

Then the fairy took off her own shoes. They were glass slippers so transparent that Cinder hadn't noticed them before.

"I can't wear those." A small knot in Cinder's stomach warned her not to take something directly from Lalyn.

"They're more comfortable than they look," said Lalyn.

Cinder hesitated, not sure if it was smart to put on a fairy's shoes. Most likely, they were just an old pair of Darlene's shoes that Lalyn had put a glamour on earlier in the day.

Cinder shrugged off the unease. The full moon and all the excitement of the ball was probably making her skittish. Anyway, it was a night for chances.

She put the glass slipper on, expecting it to be hard and clunky. At first, it was as if the shoe didn't know how to be worn by her foot. But then, as soon as she slipped her heel in, it molded itself around her foot like a sock. It fit her perfectly.

Before she knew how she felt about that, Lalyn slipped the other shoe onto Cinder's foot. The second shoe molded itself around her immediately.

The fairy gave Cinder a big smile, looking genuinely pleased.

"Have a lovely time."

Lalyn waved goodbye as she closed the carriage door with Cinder in it. Cinder watched the fairy standing beneath the rising moon as the carriage pulled away.

CHAPTER 32

The moon dominated the night. Cinder had always loved the full moon until the night of her first hunt. After that, she couldn't bear to look at it.

Now, the moon was larger than ever. A harvest moon, sitting low and heavy with a red tint to it. It looked too large to be rising over the horizon. The dark castle was silhouetted in front of it, giving the castle a soft pink glow. A foreign visitor who didn't know better might mistake it for a fairy-tale castle tonight.

Cinder took a deep breath and held it for a moment before letting it out. The hunt would be starting at midnight tonight. There had been very little talk about it this time because everyone was busy talking about the royal ball. It was sure to be a small hunt, but it would be full of the fiercest, most dedicated hunters.

Silver would be staked out in her usual spot tonight, watching for people to rescue. Cinder tried to tell herself that Silver would be all right alone tonight, but the nervousness in her belly refused to go.

Her gilded carriage rolled into the castle courtyard.

Cinder marveled at how her nervousness grew at the thought of walking into a royal ball full of people who might discover that she didn't belonged there. Silver would have scoffed at her, but that didn't change the reality of it.

It was so crowded that it took over an hour to get out of her carriage. She could have just hopped out and walked the mile it would take to get to the front entrance of the castle, but that wasn't what proper ladies did. And for tonight at least, Cinder was a proper lady.

Her stomach fluttered as she wondered if she was doing the right thing. Maybe she should turn back right now. She was sure that everyone would call her an impostor.

When it was finally time to get out of her coach, her hand trembled. She almost laughed. She could face all the tough scenarios that Silver could throw at her during training, yet she trembled at the thought of walking into a fancy party wearing a frilly dress.

A finely dressed footman helped her out with a gloved hand. She took a deep breath and gracefully exited her coach. She then walked as regally as she could into the castle.

Inside, the hall glittered with gold inlays along the walls, ceiling and even the floor. The marble beneath her feet clacked with ladies' shoes as hundreds of women gathered to be announced. One by one, they were announced at the top of a grand staircase with a steady drone of names. The guests assembled below in the ballroom occasionally took notice, but mostly, they seemed absorbed in their own merrymaking.

Cinder couldn't announce her true name, of course. So she had herself announced as Lady Fleur of the Thorn family.

Her cheeks flushed with the lie as she walked slowly down the gilded steps into the ballroom below. From there, she had a good vantage point of the crowd.

The grand ballroom was packed with towering wigs, endless yards of silk and every color of the rainbow. Men, women, girls, matrons all crowded in, trying to get the attention of the princes. Everyone seemed to know each other, or at least that was how it felt to Cinder.

She felt very alone walking down those steps. Her feet slowed as if having second thoughts of their own.

At the head of the ballroom, there stood a large throne on a red dais. It was empty, although there were two guards with spears standing like statues on either side of it. Red flags were poised beside it, and the only thing missing was the Dark King himself.

Below the dais stood two crowds of people dressed in breathtaking finery. Each crowd surrounded two young men who wore thin bands of gold around their heads. Ladies watched them with rapt attention and adoration.

In the larger group, a lady spoke to the prince. He nodded absently and turned to listen to another woman. As he turned, she got a good look at his face.

Cinder's feet stopped in mid-stride on the grand stairway.

It was Dante.

She could swear it. She blinked a few times to make sure, but he didn't change.

The other one was Gallant. Ladies spoke to him while he scanned the room with barely a nod at the women around him.

Dante and Gallant were the princes.

She had kicked mud at royalty. She had fought—

If these two were princes, then the brother she killed in the forest must have been...

The crowned prince.

The air in the room seemed to drain out. A trickle of sweat dripped down her face.

CHAPTER 33

Someone jostled her on their way past her. Cinder blinked and took deep breaths to orient herself.

She had killed the heir to the throne.

The implication of that was staggering. She gripped the stair railing, trying not to be conspicuous.

She needed to get out.

For all she knew, this whole ball could be an elaborate trap to reel in the killer of the royal heir. If they recognized her...

She turned and tried to make her way against the flow of dresses. But she only managed to take a couple of steps before trumpets blared a regal tune.

Music began playing and everyone moved back to create a space in the center of the ballroom.

In front of Cinder, the great doors of the ballroom closed at the top of the grand stairwell. Two guards stood in front of it, blocking her from leaving.

The entire crowd of guests bowed to the princes as they each chose a partner and walked out onto the dance floor.

Cinder had to turn and bow as well, otherwise, she would stand out. That was the last thing she wanted.

On the dance floor, the princes smiled at their partners, putting everyone at ease. Much to everyone's relief, there were only a few unnerving stories of the princes. People said they were both charming and handsome, as well as well mannered. It was also whispered that the princes were well adjusted, or at least one of them was. And the other one…he was as well adjusted as could be expected when his father was the Dark King.

The princes' dance partners were beautiful in a way that Cinder had never seen. She didn't recognize their fashion style and guessed that they came from far away. Their dresses were stunning, and so were their smiles.

"Enchantments," whispered a matron beside her. "Don't you worry, Millie—the princes will be jaded and familiar with cheap trickery. They'll see your natural beauty shine through all these glamours."

Millie looked like she had more than a few enchantments herself, but perhaps her mother wasn't aware of them.

Cinder had no choice but to walk down the grand stairwell away from the main doors. She couldn't just stand there until she was the only one left on the stairs. As it was, she couldn't convince her slippered feet into moving faster, so she ended up trailing the other ladies coming into the ballroom.

All the other ladies were escorted by their mamas or aunts who looked almost as young as their charges. Cinder walked faster to catch up so that she wouldn't be so noticeable.

There were plenty of men at the ball as well. Everyone knew that this was the place to be to converse with a lady who might be disappointed by the lack of royal attention. That would include most of the women in the room.

There were doors that lined one side of the ballroom leading out to a garden. She'd have to walk through much of the ball and through the dance area to reach them, but those doors were her best chance to leave.

Cinder paused when she saw her stepmother. She almost didn't recognize Helene, even though she'd seen her only a couple of hours ago. Helene looked as young as her daughters. All three were gorgeous. Lalyn had outdone herself with such finery and fashion sense.

The men around them also noticed. All three women were constantly stopped by men. At first, they turned down all the invitations to dance. But after seeing that the princes were dancing, they agreed to dance as well.

Being on the dance floor would give all the ladies a chance to smile at the princes, at least for a moment, as they danced with them during the partner-switching parts of the dance.

"Would you care to dance?" asked a young man.

Cinder looked around to make sure he was talking to her.

He smiled. "You certainly could use a dance, that is obvious. My sister is the same way. I had to practically push her onto the dance floor."

He looped his arm around hers and headed to the dance area.

She glanced up at the main ballroom doors. They were still shut and guarded. The garden doors were across the dancing area.

The young man paused. "Is this dance promised to another?"

"Not at all. I'd be happy to dance." Cinder smiled a little, trying to relax.

When she'd first entered the ballroom, she worried about being alone and unnoticed in the corner all night. Now, she wished for nothing else until she could leave.

He moved onto the dance floor, gently pulling her along.

"Excellent." He leaned in and whispered conspiratorially, "I promised Mama, who is too sick to come today, that I would look out for her baby girl. But I'm afraid some rapscallion has whisked her away. I must check in with her on the dance floor and see if she needs rescuing. You will help a poor fellow in need, won't you?"

She glanced about. Both the princes were stepping off the dance area now, surrounded by ladies and looking far too busy to notice her. The only way she'd be noticed now was if she made a scene.

She nodded. All she had to do was make it through this dance. When it ended, she could slip out into the garden.

He beamed. "My ailing mama thanks you."

He took her in his arms. It was a lovely dance.

Cinder hadn't danced since she was a little girl and had almost forgotten how much she loved it. She even smiled and forgot for a moment what sort of trouble she could be in. Sometimes, there was safety in numbers. For the moment, she felt safe that neither the princes nor her stepfamily would notice her in such a throng of people.

But then, someone tapped her partner on the shoulder.

The smile died on Cinder's face as she saw Gallant's face.

CHAPTER 34

$\mathcal{C}$inder considered running. But in this crowd, she would only make it a couple of steps before someone caught her.

The gentlemen switched places as her partner, and the prince glided effortlessly onto the dance floor with her in his arms.

"I should probably apologize for taking you away from that fine gentleman, but I couldn't help myself. All the ladies in the kingdom are here, but I find that they all look the same tonight. Strange, wouldn't you say?"

Did he recognize her? She tried to keep the tension out of her grip as she twirled on his arm.

"Then why bother to pick one over another?" she asked, trying to keep her voice low so that he might not recognize it.

"My question exactly when I happened to look up from a chittering girl, and saw my brother looking mesmerized as he watched you."

Dante was watching her?

"I thought you said we all look alike." She was surprised that her voice came out steady.

"All except you. You're the only lady wearing a mask tonight."

Her heart skipped a beat. The makeup mask that she'd thought would let her hide had only served to make her stand out in the crowd.

The prince pointed his chin to the sidelines beyond the dancers.

"See? My brother is still watching you, probably upset that he didn't get to you first. He's considering coming here, I can tell. Very rude to interrupt your elder brother during a dance to steal away his partner."

They spun, making her dress twirl.

"Is this a competition with your brother?"

"When you're in line to become king, everything is a competition. Whichever one of us chooses a wife that charms the king will inherit the entire kingdom. Is there anything more competitive than that?"

"How will you choose a wife if you can't tell one apart from another?" Cinder's mouth was dry, but she had to pretend everything was fine.

"Perhaps I'm wondering the same thing as I look at the one who is clearly different from the rest."

Heat flowed up Cinder's cheeks. She was sure that either he recognized her and was toying with her, or she seemed familiar enough to catch his attention. He was probably mistaking recognition for attraction.

"Your mask is very mysterious," he whispered in her ear.

How was she going to extract herself? Any rude or unexpected behavior would be noticed by all, including her stepfamily.

"And so are your unusual glass slippers," said Gallant as

he admired them. "I don't think I've ever seen anything like it."

Cinder caught a glimpse of her stepmother looking on with daggers in her eyes as they danced by. There was no sign of recognition, thank goodness, but naked jealousy was shining in her face.

The music stopped and the dancers paused. Cinder was breathing heavily. She'd made it through the dance without being arrested.

All she had to do now was to lose herself in the crowd as the ladies rushed over to gain the prince's attention.

She curtsied to the prince, all ready to slip away into the crowd.

"Shall we dance again?"

Cinder looked up at him like a rabbit in a snare. The crowd of ladies waiting at the edge of the dance area, most of whom still hadn't had a dance with a prince, also stared. Gallant paused rather than walk Cinder off the dance area, and the tension grew.

Gallant chuckled. "Come now, am I that much of an ogre that you look so distressed at the thought of another dance with me?"

"You are rather frightening, brother."

To Cinder's horror, Dante strode onto the dance floor toward them without a partner. He was looking right at her.

Cinder curtsied again, bowing her head to hide her face.

"Dante, find your own dance partner."

"But dear brother, if you dance twice in a row with the same lady, the other ladies will give up on you. Then I'll be left to fend for myself amongst all these beautiful women. How will I possibly choose with so many?"

"I'm sure you're up to the task," said Gallant.

"Are you truly ready to let go of all the possibilities already?" asked Dante.

"I'm not going to just let you take…" Gallant turned to Cinder. "I was so charmed by…well, your charms, that I didn't catch your name."

For a second, Cinder couldn't remember what name she had used when she was announced at the top of the stairs.

"Fleur," she said. "Lady Fleur of the Thorn family."

Dante looked at her sharply. His studied her face, looking like he was trying to figure something out.

Cinder's heart pounded. She held her hands to keep them from trembling.

"Intriguing," said Gallant. "You must tell me all about the Thorns. I don't believe I know them."

"Later, brother." Dante tore his gaze away from her and lowered his voice to a whisper. "Remember, you have a long list of ladies whose fathers regularly speak into the king's ears. These are not men either of us can afford to offend right now. You can come back later after you've danced with their daughters."

"What about you?" asked Gallant.

"I've already danced with them. I can't dance with any of them again without setting expectations."

"I'm not sure I like letting this one go to dance with you. You have a way of wanting what I have."

"Gallant." Dante's annoyance showed through his civility. "Who else in the room could cut in on your dance? I'm doing you a favor, brother."

Gallant took a deep breath. "All right. Take care of her *for me.*"

Gallant lifted Cinder's hand and kissed it before he walked away to select another dance partner.

"Shall we?" Dante put his arms out for a dance.

Dante had never seen her in this much light. Cinder desperately wished she had more than a makeup mask to hide behind. She wanted to run and hide.

Instead, she stepped into his arms and began to dance. Everyone was staring at her, curious about the girl who had managed to get both princes' attention.

It was one thing to be near Dante on a dirt road when she thought he was a nobleman's son. It was another thing altogether to be in his arms knowing he was a prince.

How could she have missed it? Now that she saw him in his element, she couldn't see him as anything other than a prince. His bearing, his confidence, his wish to be free of political agendas—it all made sense now.

CHAPTER 35

"Well," said Dante as he led her through the dance, "my brother will certainly think you're the most intriguing of all the women here now that he can't have you for this dance. I'll wager that he'll watch you like a hawk and won't let you get away tonight."

Cinder's stomach clenched.

"Not that you need anything else beyond your lovely self and that mysterious mask," he said.

He sounded somehow more princely than he did before. It was as if he had donned a political mask himself.

This was a version of Dante that was different from the one she'd seen before. This Dante was in command of the room. He could deftly nudge another prince and literally dance his way through a political quagmire.

"You're not one for conversation, are you, Lady…Thorn, was it?"

She nodded, keeping her eyes downcast. She would have danced with her head all the way down if she could so that he wouldn't see her face. She was sure he could read lies in her eyes.

"Well, Lady Thorn, I assure you that I'm not a monster. You can relax into the dance without worry that I'll throw you into the dungeons if you step on my feet."

That did not make her feel better. His hand was warm in hers, and his other hand on the small of her back felt strangely comforting. Nevertheless, the dance felt interminably long.

"I'm as curious as my brother about the Thorns. Do tell me about your family. I don't think I've met them."

She swallowed. She had no choice but to respond to a direct command from the prince.

"My father was…is…a good man." She tried to make her voice breathless so that he wouldn't give her that scrutinizing look again.

"Go on."

"He loves to laugh and read stories to…my little sister. He takes her on pony rides and sometimes, if she's really good, he'll let her ride on his shoulders. My sister doesn't have any children her age to play with, so he races with her down to the pond, although most of the time, they end up in a tickle fight on the grass."

She had to clear her throat of the tears that began to fill it. It had been years since she'd spoken of her father.

"He sounds amazing. I can't even imagine what it's like to play with one's father. Just the thought of riding on the Dark King's shoulders is enough to give a little boy nightmares." His voice was casual, but she could catch a hint of wistfulness.

"Although," he said, "I must admit that it would have been worth it just to see the faces of the nobles if the Dark King had pranced around with one of us on his shoulders. Now, tickling—that's unimaginable. Your little sister is a very fortunate girl."

"She is, your majesty."

He grinned and whispered, "That title is only for the king. Most people just call me 'my prince,' but you can call me Dante."

"I couldn't, my prince."

"You don't have to tonight if you don't want to. But eventually, I'll get you to call me by my name even if I have to kick mud at you to do it."

She stared into his eyes like a rabbit frozen in fear.

"Don't worry. I've already told you that you're safe with me."

"How did you know?"

"Your voice. I think some part of me knew even before that. I saw you as you came down the stairs. There you were, just one of many in a sea of ladies in their finest dresses, but there was something about you that caught my eye. Maybe your mask, maybe a familiar gesture, I don't know. But some part of me knew right then that I had to talk to you."

"But you waited."

He swept her in a circle in time with the music. Cinder's dress swept out along with all the other ladies' dresses on the dance floor around them.

"I was telling the truth to Gallant. I had to dance with the daughters of certain influential noblemen. I knew that if I got duty out of the way first, then I could be free to choose whomever I wanted to dance with, however many times in a row I wanted. If I had known that the mysterious girl who'd caught my eye had been you, well, I would have come to you sooner."

"Before your brother?"

"Before anybody."

The music ended. Although Cinder had earlier wished that the dance would end, she now felt reluctant to walk away from Dante.

The other dancers curtsied to their partners, and people

shuffled about, finding their next dance partners.

But Prince Dante kept a hold of Cinder's hand as he bowed. As the music began again, he pulled her closer.

Cinder's eyes widened as she fell into step with him for the next dance.

"My prince," she said, "everyone is watching."

"I know." He twirled her.

The ladies around the ballroom were talking to each other behind their fans as they watched. Helene and her daughters were throwing dagger stares at Cinder, but there was no sign of recognition.

"But everyone will think that you're considering me as your choice."

"Let them." He brought her back into his arms as she followed his lead.

Gallant glared at them with a scowl as he danced by with a blond confection of a lady in his arms.

"Look, this is not going to make it easy for me to slip out unnoticed at the end of the ball," whispered Cinder.

"Yes, I know," Dante whispered back. "I've had enough of you slipping out unnoticed at the end of the night. I think it's time that you let it ride out and see where it leads."

Cinder swallowed. Nerves of all kinds were jangling inside her. She didn't know what she was supposed to feel. There was fear, but excitement too, and anxiety along with joy. Could it be possible to feel all those things at once?

Dante spun her again, then bowed along with the rest of the men on the dance floor. He smiled as he rose to look at her. There was mischief in his eyes that she was sure had also been there when they raced on the dirt road. She would have seen it had they been laughing in the sunshine.

She couldn't help but relax and give a little smile back. She wanted to capture the moment to take out and treasure when she was back scrubbing the floor in the morning.

CHAPTER 36

*D*ante and Cinder were still dancing when trumpets blared. Everyone stopped and turned to the dais.

"His majesty the king."

The announcer took a step back, and the Dark King stepped through a door near the throne into the ballroom. He was a portly man with broad shoulders and a stout build. He had the red nose of someone who drank often, but his eyes were sharp and clear.

Everyone bowed deeply to the king. People glanced at each other beneath their eyelashes. The Dark King had a way of unnerving people.

He stood before the crowd in his famous cloak. It was trimmed in luxurious fur, but Cinder could see the seams where the material had been sewn together from large patches of hide. The patches were mostly various shades ranging from light tan to dark leather, but there were a few patches that were a dull blue or green.

People said that it was made of the skin of fairies that he'd slain during the Wild Wars. The elders who'd lived through the wars whispered that only a few of the patches were actually fairy skin. The rest were from his human enemies.

"Welcome," said the king.

He sounded like he meant it. Cinder had always heard that the king rarely sounded enthusiastic about anything that didn't involve fresh blood.

"This is a fine group of ladies," said the king. "And lords, of course." He nodded to the men. "As you all know, tonight is the full moon. I have a surprise for those of you who are participating in the hunt, as well as for those ladies who are here tonight."

He smiled. Everyone knew that bad things happened when the Dark King smiled.

"Since there is only so much time in a person's life—even a king's—sometimes, we must combine two lovely activities to fit it all in. Tonight, as I have suspected, my sons are having a difficult time getting beyond the fairy glamours. I have told them that the one who chooses wisely will be my heir. Yet how are they to choose wisely when the ladies are so clever?"

He smiled again and looked down on his subjects.

"The solution is this—the great ball and the great hunt shall be combined."

The crowd looked around in confusion. Everyone already knew that many of the noblemen would leave for the hunt at midnight. Most assumed they would come back in a few hours, especially since neither of the princes had announced their choice.

"All the fairy slaves in the land were secretly commanded to make their glamours last only until midnight."

The crowd erupted with noise as ladies made shocked sounds. Who knew what they looked like beneath their glamours?

"Then we shall see what the ladies here are truly like," said the king. "I hope you ladies are wearing sturdy shoes beneath those laces, because I don't want simpering tricksters in my bloodline. I want warriors. Survivors. Grandchildren who can tear the fairy kingdom out from its very roots."

The Dark King made a fist and hammered down on his other hand.

"The fine ladies here tonight will be given until midnight to run, to hide, to do whatever it is that fine ladies do in the forest on a full moon."

The Dark King smiled at his guests.

"Then the hunt shall begin. The princes will choose from the survivors."

CHAPTER 37

The ballroom boomed with the sound of closing doors. The doors leading out to the garden slammed shut, all at once. Guards stood in front of each, armed with their swords.

"Ladies, I suggest you exit through that door." The king gestured to the only open door in the room. "Anyone who is left when the midnight bell tolls will be fair game."

A collective gasp went through the room.

"Hunters, don your masks. It is, after all, a festive occasion."

One of the doors opened, and a procession of servants carrying trays laden with golden masks of beasts and monsters began walking toward the king.

The ballroom filled with screams as everyone panicked. A mad rush to the door at the far end of the ballroom began.

Many of the men stood in confusion as the women cried and pushed their way toward the door. More than a few of the men looked dazedly around, looking like they needed someone to guide them and tell them what to do. They were just as surprised as the ladies.

Cinder could see that it would take too long to get all the way over to the far door. That part of the ballroom was quickly being mobbed by panicked people.

Servants circulated around the ballroom with their trays. Most of the men refused the masks, but one out of every four or five took one and slid it over his face. The king nodded to each of those men.

Cinder's eyes met Dante's. He seemed as surprised as she was, but he recovered fast.

"My father usually takes his entertainment very seriously."

He looped his arm in hers and spun her toward one of the guarded doors.

"I suggest you come with me," he said. "You'll never make it out in time."

Cinder followed the prince on numb feet.

A part of her noticed that a few of the couples also approached side doors and spoke to the guards. They were firmly turned away. Some ran back into the exiting crowd, but a couple of others made heated demands, declaring how important they were. The rest brought out bags of gold and dangled them in front of the guards.

Dante and Cinder slipped out of one of the side doors without any objection from the guards. Apparently, they didn't have the nerve to say no to a royal prince.

Outside, the night was silent. The ladies of the dark kingdom knew instinctively how to behave like prey, and they stayed quiet.

A steady stream of ladies in ball gowns flowed out of the castle and were corralled into the forest. A few tried to escape the woods, but the forest snagged them as they tried to pass the border.

The attempted escapees got tangled in roots and vines. They ran into huge cobwebs that they couldn't escape from.

They tripped and got dragged down by something that wouldn't let go as they struggled against getting sucked all the way down into the soil.

It was as if the forest had joined in the hunt, refusing to let the prey out of its boundaries.

The others saw this and followed the line of guards into the woods. Several of them whispered about enchantments and hugged themselves on the way in.

Many of the women were crying, with dark streaks running down their cheeks. Several of them had taken their wigs off, making their heads look scrawny, like bald chicks.

Cinder saw one twist her ankle on the way into the forest, but the guards shoved her into the thicket anyway.

Dante rushed Cinder into the shadows and skirted the crowd.

"Prince, help us!" yelled a young lady.

But she wasn't calling to Dante. She had her hands out in supplication to Gallant.

Gallant walked by the crowd of ladies, looking for someone. The girl watched him with hope in her eyes. But her mother beside her seemed to have no delusions about what the princes would and could do against their king.

Gallant looked away from the begging girl. He looked like he was both avoiding looking at the ladies who were being shoved into the woods, and at the same time scanning the crowd for someone.

"My prince," said a guard trotting up to Dante and Cinder. It was the guard who had let them through the door.

"The king commands that the princes be by his side at the start of the hunt."

The hunt was about to begin.

Cinder could almost smell a change in the air. Everyone seemed to be breathing harder, more labored, including Dante. He squeezed Cinder's arm and bowed to her.

"My apologies, my lady," said Dante. "I'm afraid this is as far as I can go to help you."

He looked deep into her eyes. For a moment, Cinder thought she saw something shift in his eyes. A shadow crossing over him.

People talked about the hunt calling out to the hunters as though it was a living thing. Cinder shivered at the thought.

The moment passed, and he shook his head and turned. He and the guard disappeared back into the shadows toward the castle.

Cinder ran as lightly as she could, hoping to find a hole in the chain of soldiers that trapped both her and the other women. No such luck. At some point, she'd have to run out of the shadow and into the moonlit field between the castle and the woods.

"Hey! What are you doing out of line?" a soldier called out from the field. He was walking toward her.

Cinder froze.

Another soldier walked toward her from another direction. Now that she'd been noticed, several soldiers looked over at her.

She braced for a fight, but she didn't have much of a chance against the king's army. So she didn't resist when a soldier grabbed her arm and shoved her toward the stream of women rushing into the forest.

"Don't you know your best chance is in the forest?" whispered the soldier. "Don't try to get out until sunrise. Run and hide in the woods as far away from here as you can."

He was trying to help. He might even have a sister in the crowd. The ball had been open to all—highborn and common.

Cinder had no choice but to run into the forest along with the rest of the women.

Once there, though, it was as if the air changed. The

woods were eerily lit with moonlight filtering into places it shouldn't.

Cinder began to shiver. She was back in the hunt.

She had to take deep breaths and practice the focusing techniques that Silver had taught her so that she wouldn't freeze in fear. She felt the cold air filling her lungs and noticed the tightness of her muscles. The mere noticing loosened her muscles enough to let her run through the forest without being clumsy.

The women clustered together and ran in one direction, following each other. Cinder tried to tell them to split up, but no one listened.

"We'll be easy prey if we stick together," said Cinder. "We'll trample a track a mile wide. We're better off all going our own separate ways."

"But then we'll be alone," said the woman nearest her. Her shimmery gown was already torn and dirty. "They won't kill all of us, not if we're all together."

"Listen. I've been through a hunt before."

The women near Cinder gasped. It was unheard of for a lady of any respectability to be forced to go through a hunt— at least, until now.

"I've been hunted, and I've survived. Splitting up is your best chance. Otherwise, you'll be caught as soon as the clock stops ringing."

As soon as she said that, the clock tower started ringing.

The first bell of midnight.

Cinder let the others do what they wanted and ran deeper into the woods, away from the rest of the hunted. She didn't know if anyone followed her. All she knew was the panic.

The nobles would be turning in the ballroom—from civilized noblemen to masked monsters. She imagined them dropping their embroidered coats and trampling over them on their way out of the ballroom to hunt their prey.

Twelve times the bell rang, each time feeling like the last.

After that, all Cinder could hear was her heart pounding in her ears.

CHAPTER 38

*J*ust as the last bell tolled, Cinder's clothes changed. Her dress changed back into Darlene's old dress. Her fan and dance card thudded onto the ground as they turned back into her old boots.

Boots.

Cinder quickly shoved off Lalyn's shoes and laced on her boots. As a last-minute thought, she grabbed Lalyn's glass slippers and shoved them into her dress pockets. But the pockets were so small that one of the shoes fell out. Cinder didn't have time to look for it.

She ran as fast and as far as she could—through the stream, over the fallen logs, past the whispering leaves and deep into the enchanted forest.

It wasn't long before the wolfkin began howling.

Screams came to her right, so she veered to the left, trying not to think about those women. She couldn't help them. She'd be lucky if she could help herself.

Someone whispered among the trees.

But when she turned to look, nobody was there. The fairies and beasts of the forest were playing tricks on her.

She wanted to hit something. It was bad enough that hunters were after her. Did she need to deal with spiteful sprites as well?

That made her so angry that she kicked a rock into a tree. "Ouch!"

Cinder stopped, trying to calm her breathing so that she could hear who said that.

"No wonder they're after you. Let them get you, I say. What do I care?"

"Who said that?"

A grumbling creature stood up on two legs and walked away from her. He had broad shoulders that were so hunched that he looked like a boulder on legs. An impossibly tattered men's shirt the color of dirt draped over his form. He dragged a broad stick behind him even though he was only half of Cinder's height.

"Hello? I'm sorry I kicked a stone at you. I didn't know you were there."

"No one ever does." He stopped but didn't turn to look at Cinder.

"Can you help me find a good place to hide for the night?"

He turned to look at her. "Why would I give away one of my hiding spots to you? You'll likely come back in daylight and poke sticks at me when I'm not myself."

"Not yourself?"

Then understanding flooded into her. She'd heard old stories of creatures like him. Children's fables that never quite seemed true, but she hadn't been able to abandon them as not true, either.

"Right," she said. "The full moon. This is your full-moon body. You're a different pers—uh, creature—the rest of the time. Am I right?"

He cocked his head. "How do you know that I won't eat you?"

"I'm guessing that you already would have if you were going to."

"Maybe I'm not hungry now but will be soon, after I've led you to my lair."

"Maybe. But if you were to do that, you wouldn't be so stupid as to tell me about it."

"You bother me," he said. "You can starve in the woods." He turned and walked away from her.

"Wait. I won't starve in the woods. The hunters will find me first. Will you at least point me in the right direction to a good hiding area? Lalyn the fairy did at least that much for me."

He stopped in his tracks and looked back at her.

"Lalyn the fairy?" he whispered. "She spoke to you directly?"

His eyes were wide, and he looked around as if afraid of being overheard. Cinder looked around too but saw only tall trees with moonlight streaming between them.

He smacked his head a couple of times with his gnarled hand. "Is it time? Has a prince been caught?"

"Caught? Do you mean have they picked their brides? That's the last thing anybody cares about right now. Can you please help me?"

"Why do you need my help? If you can kill the hunters the way you have in the past, you shouldn't need me."

Cinder was very still. "What did you say?"

"Oh, I have eyes. I see things."

She didn't know what to say to that. She had to clear her throat of the dryness before saying anything.

"Have you been following me?" she asked.

"Only because I was commanded to, not because you interest me in any way. Why else would I do anything at all other than eat, sleep, and… Well, you get my meaning."

"Who told you to follow me?"

He looked around secretively. "I'm nobody's slave, you see."

"Who?"

"It's just that, sometimes, I forget what happens on the full moon. Forget who I am and all that. She told me that she could make me remember everything if I only did something for her on those full moons."

"So you struck a bargain." Lalyn was a firm believer in bargains.

He nodded.

Cinder mouthed the fairy's name without making a sound.

He looked around furtively and nodded again.

"Why?"

"I told you. I didn't remember—"

"I know, but why did she want you to follow me?"

He shrugged. "It was all part of the plan."

"What plan?"

"Didn't ask." He shook his head with his eyes closed. Then he peeked his eyes open with a sly look. "But I did follow."

"Me?"

He nodded. "And her. On nights when it wasn't the full moon. I reported to her what you did on the hunt nights. But to do that, she had to let me remember everything. So I remembered." A tragic look crossed his face. "Some things, you just shouldn't know, you know?"

He wiped his nose with a sniffle.

"I was a fine young man in the village. I had a wife and two children who loved me. I had friends and parents."

A tear streaked down his face. "But once I learned what I became on the full moons, I got it into my thick head that they needed to know too. My lovely wife. My wonderful children. My friends. My parents."

He wiped his eyes again with his hairy arm.

"I'm sorry."

Perhaps it had had been different before the war, but for as long as Cinder had been alive, the villagers weren't known for their tolerance of people who were different. And this little creature was definitely different.

"I've lost them all." His voice wavered. "Now, even on nights that aren't full moons, I live here, in the dark forest."

"Couldn't you try to live in the world again? You're…like the rest of us on all the other nights."

"Once you know that you're different, you can't *un*know. And you can't ever go back."

She just nodded because she couldn't figure out what else to say.

He sighed. "I followed you. Now it's time for you to follow me." He began walking.

Not knowing what to do or where to go, Cinder followed.

CHAPTER 39

*C*inder and the creature walked for what seemed like hours. It was punctuated by them hiding from hunters riding through the forest or screams echoing through the night.

Once, they walked far too close to a pack of wolfkin growling and snapping over a kill. Cinder and the troll froze in their tracks. But it turned out that the beasts were occupied enough that Cinder and the troll could nervously sneak past the feeding frenzy.

Cinder tried to concentrate only on escaping the forest alive. She knew there was no getting out while the moon was out. Even though she didn't see anyone else trapped on the edge of the forest, it was too risky. The entire forest was probably enchanted tonight, so she'd have to wait until sunrise.

"How long until sunrise?" she asked as she pushed branches out of the way.

"Hours still, a lifetime away. Besides, be careful what you ask for."

"Why would you say that? All of this nightmare will go away after the sun rises."

He glanced back at her with a mysterious look. "Which nightmare is worse, I wonder?"

Horses whinnied far too close.

Cinder and the creature dropped onto the forest floor and froze.

Ahead of them, three hunters wearing masks slipped off their horses and surrounded a girl and an older lady. The girl was no more than thirteen, while the lady must have been her grandmother.

"What have we here?" The first hunter circled the females, looking them up and down.

All three of the hunters wore golden wolf masks. Otherwise, they still wore their noblemen's finery from the ball.

"They couldn't even be bothered with charms to make them an appropriate age for our princes," said the second hunter.

"Their glamours wore off, cousin," said the third hunter. "These two were trying to fool the princes into marrying them. Just imagine our kingdom with a child and grandmother queens ruling the land."

"Ugly ones at that," said the first.

One of them picked up dung from below his horse and smeared it across the grandmother's face.

They laughed. The grandmother looked down at their feet, careful not to enrage them. Cinder didn't think it mattered what she did. The hunters would do whatever they felt like doing.

"That's what you get for trying to fool everyone."

"But the Dark King invited everyone to use fairy magic," said the girl with tears in her voice.

The second hunter mimicked her high-pitched whine.

"And the Dark King invited us to do whatever we liked to those who tried to fool his sons."

He paced around far too close to the girl, shoving her with his body so that she shifted this way and that as he circled her.

The third hunter shoved his wolf-masked face into hers. "Anything we want."

He lifted his mask and spat in her eyes.

The grandmother put her arm around the girl's shoulder and pulled her to her side.

Cinder couldn't bear to watch. But neither could she fight off three grown men. They were also so close that she couldn't get away without catching the hunter's attention. She and the creature were stuck witnessing whatever happened so long as the hunters chose to do it here.

She couldn't do it.

Her blood boiled. What was the point of all those years of training if not to fight off hunters like these?

Silver's voice told her to always run when she could, and only fight if she had no choice. She'd drilled that into Cinder's head for years now.

Cinder's hand shook with the intensity of her anger, though. She wanted to rend the hunters with her bare hands, to pound them into jelly with the biggest rock she could find.

She shut her eyes and let the feeling consume her.

The young girl began screaming.

Cinder's brain argued with her body, begged her to think of her own survival. There were three of them and only one of her. Each of the three were stronger than her, and well armed as well.

She grabbed a nearby rock and leapt up. She roared as she catapulted into the men.

She lifted her hand and swung it to pummel the one who had grabbed the girl.

But a hand caught hers in mid-swing.

Someone else punched her from the side.

She fell onto the ground and felt a heavy weight on top of her.

Panic.

She hadn't even gotten a single hit in before she was overwhelmed. This wasn't working the way she envisioned.

Of course not, her brain yelled. *Stupid. Stupid. Stupid.*

The voice in her brain was Silver's. Hard without mercy. That voice drove Cinder, step by step, into the kind of violence she couldn't remember practicing.

Like an animal, her mouth was the first thing she used. She bit into her attacker's throat and clamped down as hard as she could.

She freed her hands and went right for his eyes. He tried to stop her, but his strength seemed to be flagging by the second.

There were screams. Hers sounded like an animal's; his sounded like prey.

Cinder had no sense of time, no sense of who or what was near her. Her entire world filled with her enemy. His breathing, his screaming, his blood in her mouth, his slippery and weakly grasping hands as she bit and tore, snarled and snapped.

Then the screams stopped.

Cinder got up slowly, looking at the blood on her hands. She was covered in blood—on her chest, her hands, her torso. She could feel it dripping down her chin.

What had come over her?

She sucked in ragged, animal breaths.

Finally, she could take in what was happening around her.

The troll, if that was what he was, stood over the second

hunter, pounding a cudgel into him, pulverizing his head into jelly.

The third hunter lay dead near her. Mauled and torn apart. Standing over him was the biggest wolfkin she'd ever seen. It was larger than a wolf, but it moved like one.

It looked up with its disturbingly intelligent eyes. Pulling back its bloody muzzle, it growled at her.

Cinder froze.

There was nothing she could do to protect herself from it should it decide to attack.

Then a sharp whistle rang through the woods. The beast looked up at the sound and waited.

A man strode out toward them. Dressed in finery, he looked like the other hunters except he wasn't wearing a mask.

Dante.

She blinked a couple of times to make sure she was seeing what she was seeing.

CHAPTER 40

*D*ante offered a hand to help her up.

Cinder hesitated. Shame blanketed her, and she didn't want to bring notice to the blood on her hands.

So she put her hands on the ground and pushed herself up without reaching up to him.

"Are you going to attack me too?" she asked, looking nervously at the enormous wolfkin.

"He won't hurt you." Dante pointed into the woods, and the beast ran off like a silent ghost.

"I always thought that a wolfkin attacked uncontrollably." She wiped the sweat off her brow. At least she hoped it was sweat.

"They're a special breed," he said. "They're hunters and killers, but they can be controlled, at least up to a point."

He looked at the carnage surrounding them. The troll stood over his kill with his cudgel dripping blood.

"Are you all right?" asked Dante.

"I'm alive," said Cinder.

"Not all men are beasts, you know."

"I didn't say they were. Many are prey in these woods,

trying to rescue their daughters and sisters. It's the hunters who are beasts."

He brushed by her to get a good look at the hunter she'd mauled. Mauled was a good word for it, wasn't it?

She looked at her hands again. She needed to wash the blood off. She didn't want to wipe it on her dress. She didn't want to carry any more on her.

Neither Cinder nor Dante were natural killers, but Midnight eventually broke everyone unless they chose a dark path. It looked like the path for them was the darkest of all.

She really needed to clean the blood off her. They had passed over a stream a few yards back.

"I'm going to wash up."

She walked away, dazed at what had just happened.

The grandmother and girl were nowhere in sight. Good. They were smart enough to run instead of sticking around to see who won. The troll had slinked away, but Cinder was sure he was watching.

Cinder dipped her hands in the cold water, wondering if this kind of life had always been meant for her. Was she like this when her father was alive?

She cupped water into her hands and poured it over her head. Then she splashed as much of it as she could onto herself to get as clean as she could.

It was no use. She could wash the blood off her skin, but not her clothes or hair.

She was a killer once again.

"I'd like to say it gets easier, but it doesn't," said Dante.

He walked over to her and dipped his bloody sword into the stream. She didn't ask whose blood that was. He bent over and gently splashed water on it.

"It just gets more common," he said. "You stop thinking about it every moment of your life. But it's always there, in the back of your mind. Every time someone tells you that you're nice or kind or worthy, it comes back to you."

"This isn't my first kill."

She splashed more water on her face, scrubbing it as best she could. "And he deserved it. All the hunters deserve it."

"Does that include me?" He dipped his hands into the water and rubbed them.

"Are you a hunter tonight?"

He grimaced. "I am *the* hunter tonight."

"Why do you participate? You're a prince. You don't have to do anything you don't want to."

"It's the king's command. Even a prince must obey the king." He wouldn't meet her eyes.

"And?"

He looked up at her. "And some of us enjoy the hunt."

"You don't."

"How do you know? I have my father's blood running through my veins. It seems my entire family is full of blood-lust, so why not me?" He sounded sad.

"Because that's not who you are."

"That's who I'm supposed to be if I want to be the heir to the throne."

"Says who?"

"My father, the king."

"Do you really want to be that kind of king?"

He laughed. "You know, no one has ever asked me the kind of questions you ask. The nobles are too terrified to question royalty."

"Sorry. I forget who I'm talking to sometimes. I guess out here, I can't help but think of you as just Dante, the boy I can always outrun in a race."

"Your head is full of fantasies, I see."

"Yes, but that doesn't change how I see you...or who you actually are."

"I sometimes forget who I am too." His voice was wistful. "Not too often. Mostly when I'm with you."

"You sound like you actually want to forget that you're a prince."

"Even princes can become trapped."

"I always thought a prince could do whatever he wanted."

He snorted. "And I always thought a peasant could do whatever she wanted."

Now it was her turn to snort.

"By royal command, my brother and I are to hunt down our wives. Hunt them down like animals in the forest." It was clear by his tone that he was disgusted by the idea.

She paused in her washing and looked over at him. "And do what with them?"

"Marry them, of course."

She barked a laugh. "That's your courtship? You expect her to fall in love with you as you hunt her down like a rabid dog?"

"Love has nothing to do with it."

"Obviously. Then what are your criteria? Why not just randomly pick someone and leave the rest of us out of your miserable courtship?"

"First, there's the entertainment value."

"For who? Certainly not for the ladies."

"For my father, the king. It's not just the ladies who provide entrainment. If Damon were still alive and this had been his time to marry, a hunt would not have been necessary."

"Why not?"

"My older brother was cruel. He enjoyed the hunt. A courtship like this would have been a treat for him. That would have been far from entertaining to the Dark King."

"So if Damon had still been alive, the king would have commanded a romantic courtship for him?"

"Without a doubt. That would have been torture for Damon."

"And for you?"

He sighed. "For me and Gallant, the torture is having our future wives be run down in the forest. We are meant to spend the night knowing we are responsible for all the harm that comes to the ladies of the realm, from the poorest milk-maid to the noblest cousin."

"Does that torture you?"

He looked into her eyes. "Wouldn't it torture you?"

She looked back down at her bloody sleeves and tried to squeeze as much of the stain out as possible.

"And how are you expected to find your wife?"

"By finding one in her natural form, devoid of all her glamour, and guarding her until sunrise. My father knew that every woman would enter the castle gates secure in her glamour. She would likely not have bothered with real preparation with neither her appearance nor who they truly were inside as a person. Once the glamour was stripped, she'd have nothing but her true self."

"Is it so important to find one without her glamour?"

"When my father had Damon's mother executed, she cursed him and all his heirs to be enslaved by fairy magic. Damon would be the only exception. Whether she yelled her curse as a desperate attempt at bargaining with her king, or as a real curse, no one knows. The story was kept quiet with only a few members of the court knowing about it. But my father has been afraid of fairy magic ever since. And now with Damon gone, his fear grows every day."

"That's why he's so dedicated about hunting fairies and enslaving them?"

"Yes. He is afraid that one or both of his sons will marry under the spell of a fairy. He'd kill the fairies if he could, but he hasn't figured out how."

"He killed the Fairy Queen. That's how he won the war, right?"

He didn't answer. But none was needed. Everyone knew that story.

"He thinks he can get around the curse by convincing the brides-to-be to rely on glamour," she said, "and then stripping them of it in the woods so he knows what he's really getting?"

"Exactly."

"But true fairy magic can be stronger than that."

Cinder looked down at the glass slipper peeking out from her apron pocket. It was clear and clean, as though no blood had ever touched it.

"Which is why my father used trickery. If everyone thinks that cheap glamour is enough, everyone would use it. Why go through the cost and hassle of real magic when easy magic is enough?"

Cinder absent-mindedly squeezed blood out of her hem as she thought about what he'd said.

"My father not only wants us to marry without trickery, he wants strength in his bloodline."

"Someone who can survive the hunt."

He nodded. "That, and I suspect it also pleases him to know that we all suffer at least for a few hours. He enjoys it when he can cause pain in the guise of it being good for us."

They both sat quietly for a moment, washing the blood off themselves.

"You are as trapped as I am," said Cinder.

"If only we could run away."

"You'd leave an entire kingdom behind?"

"It's not my kingdom. My father has seen to it that his will be carried out even after one of us takes the throne."

"What would you do if you were no longer a prince?"

He shrugged. "Be a scholar? I can write letters for people.

Or teach. Be a minstrel? I love music. I'm sure I'm quite talented, too." He smiled.

"Of course. And I could play the tambourine by your side."

"And tell fortunes."

She smiled. "I don't know anything about telling fortunes."

"It's all right. I don't know anything about being a minstrel."

"I suppose it wouldn't matter because everyone in Everness is kind and generous. We would have no troubles getting by."

"Oh, we'd be going to Everness, now, would we?"

"Where else would we go but to the land of sunshine and laughter?"

They listened to the sound of the stream for a while. They both knew there was no such place. And even if there were, one would have to trek through the forest to get there or to any other kingdom, real or imagined.

"Do you know the way out of Midnight?" she asked.

"No. My father is afraid that his sons will conspire against him with his enemies if they could go in and out of the kingdom at will. Only the new king will find out."

Cinder nodded, unsurprised. The night was getting chilly and they couldn't sit by the stream forever, but neither of them were in a rush to end the moment of peace.

Cinder leaned over to pull her dress out of the way so it would not drag in the water. When she did, a glass slipper fell out of her apron pocket.

"What's that?" The prince was looking intently at the shoe.

Cinder collected it. "It was for my ball gown. I figured I didn't need it once the clock tower began ringing."

"May I see it?" Dante reached over.

Cinder put the shoe in his hand. He seemed wary, as if it was far more than a shoe.

Behind them, the troll hissed. "Fairy gifts."

Cinder glanced at the troll. How long had he been there?

The prince looked up at the troll and lifted his sword.

"It's all right," said Cinder. "He's a friend. Sort of."

Dante took a moment before lowering his sword. He studied the shoe with a frown.

"Gallant is looking for the lady who fits this shoe."

Cinder cocked her head. "Why would your brother be doing that?"

"He thinks he's found his wife. He declares that he's madly in love and has claimed her for himself. I've promised to stay away from her."

"What does that have to do with the shoes?"

"He's not sure what she looks like without her glamour. He found one in the woods and swears she had been wearing it at the ball. So he's looking for the girl who fits in the shoe."

Cinder patted her pockets for the other shoe and found them as empty as her stomach. Her cheeks burned and she had trouble meeting the prince's gaze.

"Are these yours?" There was tension in his voice.

"Well, not exactly."

His shoulders relaxed.

"I mean, I wore them to the ball, but they're borrowed."

The prince's nostrils flared.

"They're the fairy's," the troll said.

The prince's brow furrowed. "Fairy?"

"What will your brother do if he finds the person who fits the shoe?" Cinder asked.

Dante stared into her eyes. "Marry her."

Cinder's mind spun. She stood up abruptly.

"We must find him before the fairy does. She fits the shoe."

CHAPTER 41

They ran from the stream in the direction Dante last saw his brother.

Along the way, they met up with two groups of hunters. The prince protected Cinder and fended off the other hunters.

Cinder was happy to let him. She was still shaken up by the viciousness with which she had fought earlier. Everyone knew the full moon made people do strange and violent things, but she didn't want to experience that again.

The hunters didn't put up a fight. They were more interested in finding their own quarry than stealing the prince's.

Nobles had learned that royalty had a way of remembering all the insults that happened to them, no matter how many years passed. So although the Dark King had commanded the hunters to steal the women that the princes protected, the hunters were timid in their approach and were happy to avoid confrontation with one of the two possible future kings.

By the time Cinder, Dante and the troll found Gallant, it was almost dawn.

He stood by the edge of the forest with a charmed smile on his face. He looked enchanted with the lady in front of him. It seemed impossible to get his attention away from her, no matter how much Dante called his name as they ran toward him.

"Enchanted," huffed Dante as they ran.

"Not by magic," said the troll.

"In love?" asked Cinder as she scampered over a fallen tree.

The first ray of light hit the couple before the three could reach them. Gallant and the lady stepped over the boundary of the forest and into the pink and gold dawn.

Outside the forest, a crowd of people cheered. They stood among colorful flags that flapped in the wind. A line of heralds dressed in royal crimson provided much fanfare as the sound of their trumpets filled the air. The king himself stepped forward to embrace the couple in his ample arms.

Cinder, Dante and the troll watched from the edge of the still-dark forest. The morning light took longer to penetrate the woods, and none of them were inclined to walk out into the crowd.

Gallant looked so happy as he embraced his father and looked at his beloved. It was as if he had finally gotten everything he had dreamt of.

It was a fairytale picture of love and royalty. A handsome prince, his newfound love and his approving father, the king. They would tell tales of this happy moment for generations to come.

Cinder's heart went out to him. It was all a lie.

She yelled a warning out to him, but no one heard her over the cheers of the crowd. The new heir to the throne kissed his betrothed.

Cinder watched the woman beside Gallant. Her skin was smooth and her eyes sparkled like jewels. Her long hair shone like gold in the dawn light, and her lips were as red as an apple in season.

Cinder had never seen Lalyn so beautiful and glowing. She looked genuinely happy.

"Now, she will be queen of both the forest and the kingdom," said the troll.

He sounded sad. The poor creature looked tortured as he watched the handsome prince kiss the beautiful Lalyn.

Cinder glanced at the prince beside her. He had lost his chance at inheriting the kingdom. But he looked more concerned about the trickery than concerned about not being heir. If anything, she guessed he might have felt some relief.

"We could go and demand their attention." She brought out her glass slipper. "We could prove that Lalyn is a fairy who planned all this. She must have used me to lure Gallant."

"Either of the princes would have sufficed," said the troll. "She knew you were her best bet, since you had caught the attention of both the princes." He shrugged. "She did make other bets, though. Lalyn doesn't like to lose."

Dante shook his head as he watched his brother. "Now that the betrothal is public, there is nothing we can do."

"You could tell Gallant the truth."

They both watched Gallant. He looked happy and in love.

"He'd never listen to me. He'd accuse me of being jealous, of trying to wrestle the throne away from him."

"What about your father?"

He thought about it for a moment, then shook his head.

"He's announced his heir. To rescind it, the king would have to admit that not only was Gallant fooled, but that he himself was fooled as well. He cannot do that without losing control of his kingdom and having his enemies call him an old, doddering man."

"Maybe he'd assassinate Lalyn or imprison her and just tell the world that she died in an accident?"

The troll snorted. "Never happen. 'Accidents' don't happen to Lalyn."

They all watched the crowd. They cheered on the new couple as the surviving nobles stiffly congratulated the royal couple. No one seemed to remember that there was another prince still somewhere in the forest.

"So what happens now?" asked Cinder.

Dante turned to look at her. In his eyes was a fire that almost frightened her in its intensity.

"Come with me. Let's run away from all this. After what happened last night and this morning, no one will notice that we're gone. Even if they did, no one would care. We could go and start a new life in a new place."

"Where?"

Excitement built in Cinder's chest. She knew she'd say yes regardless of the answer.

The prince glanced into the woods. He didn't know either.

"I know of a place," said the troll.

"Why haven't you gone there?" asked Cinder.

"Because I was commanded to watch you."

"By whom?" asked Dante.

"Lalyn."

"Why?" asked Dante.

"She owes the girl. She commanded me to watch over her, and when Lalyn won this game by being selected by the prince, I was to give the girl safe passage through the forest."

"To go where?"

"Wherever she wants."

"How do we know this isn't a trick?" asked Dante.

"Lalyn doesn't want to owe debts to anyone. If you'll agree," said the troll to Cinder, "then I shall guide you through the woods, and you shall have safe passage. No beast or wild fairy will harm you. Do you agree to accept this payment for all the debt she owes you?"

"What debts are these?" asked Cinder.

"Freeing her from the barn in which she was imprisoned when she was bonded to a wraith horse, giving her food and clothes and all the other little favors you foisted onto her whether she wanted them or not."

Cinder and Dante looked at each other with the wonder in their eyes. The troll knew the way through the forest. Out into the wide world.

Freedom.

CHAPTER 42

"Where—" Cinder began to ask. But she knew the answer before she finished her question.

"Everness," both she and Dante said at the same time.

"Can you take us to Everness?" Cinder asked the troll.

The troll wrinkled his nose but nodded.

Cinder gave a small gasp. Goosebumps prickled along her arms.

"It's real then?" she asked.

The troll sneered but nodded.

Cinder and Dante exchanged another glance full of cautious wonder. Dante had more caution than wonder in his eyes, but it was there nevertheless.

"Is it full of sunshine and laughter, like they say?" she asked.

"Don't know," grumbled the troll. "I don't go near it, but I know where it is. I can take you as far as I can, then point you in the right direction."

That by itself told Cinder and Dante enough to decide.

"What about Lalyn?" asked Dante.

The troll shrugged. "Someone will kill her for her

betrayal to her kind. Most fairies are disgusted by a joining with humans. Or they may enslave her and sell her to her own precious humans. Cut her up and feed her to her half-breed children. It matters not."

Cinder was surprised at the coldness of the troll's words. The prince, who perhaps was no longer a prince, seemed unsurprised, though. She supposed he was used to such cold talk of war.

"Will you give up the throne so easily?" she asked Dante.

"There is nothing I can do short of attacking with an army. Since I have no army, I either find a different occupation or build up an army."

"Both can be found in the new land if you're clever enough," said the troll.

The prince nodded. He reached up and took the crown off his head.

Beyond the forest's edge, the cheering crowd began to move away from the woods as the happy couple headed to the castle.

On the fringes of the crowd, Cinder caught sight of Helene and the stepsisters. They were all wearing the tattered, patched-up dresses that used to be Cinder and Lalyn's. Cinder had forgotten that those old dresses had been the starting point for the enchanted ball gowns.

Helene and the stepsisters did not fare well during the hunt, although they survived. They tried to back up and scamper off into the alleys of Midnight, never to be seen again, but found they couldn't.

They had built up quite a debt with Lalyn, and she wasn't the kind of fairy to forget her debts. So Cinder's fake stepfamily found themselves the Fairy Queen's servants.

Cinder and her own prince watched her stepfamily be dragged behind the royal couple's procession as they all walked up to the castle.

"Shall we set off to our new home, Cinder?"

The prince looked very handsome in his finery. Gold threads shone on his chest, and his silk collar looked clean and bright.

Escape into a new life with her handsome prince? Why not? A new life and new adventures awaited them. They could face it together.

Cinder nodded with a happy smile.

"Yes, my prince. Yes!"

She laughed as he lifted her up in his arms and swung her in a circle.

When he put her down, she said, "But first, we need to find my friend Silver and take her with us."

"I must lead you through the forest and come back to Lalyn as soon as I can," said the troll. "So do what you must but be quick about it."

Cinder left Dante with the troll so that she wouldn't give away Silver's hiding spot in the woods. Cinder raced through the trees, hoping she didn't miss Silver. She preferred not to be out in town if she could help it. Who knew what might happen once she left the woods?

Silver was gathering her cache of weapons to leave when Cinder found her.

"You're alive, then," said Silver as she slung her bow over her shoulder.

"Silver, we're leaving. Me and..." Cinder had to smile because she couldn't believe what she was saying. "And one of the princes."

Silver's brows shot up. "Really? And where might you and your princeling go?"

Cinder took a deep breath. "Everness."

Silver's expression shifted just a touch—still stoic, but cautious, as if she knew something that others didn't. Not belief, but not disbelief either.

"It's a long story," said Cinder. "We have to go now. I'll tell you all about it along the way."

"You're sure this is what you want to do?"

"If there's a shot at freedom and happiness, we have to take it. Let's go."

"My path lies a different way."

"What? You want to stay here? In this horrible place full of monsters? Selling flowers to people who hunt villagers and be ruled by a twisted maniac of a king?"

Silver smiled a little. "Well, when you put it that way, it does sound foolish, doesn't it?"

She embraced Cinder in a big hug.

"My life is committed to a cause, child. And that cause is greater than my desire for comforts."

Cinder held Silver's hands. "You can't rescue enough people to make a difference. The hunt will continue."

"I'm not talking about the hunt. I'm talking about the war."

"Silver, the Wild Wars are over. They've been over for most of my life."

"I'm not talking about the wars of the past. I'm talking about the war that's going on right now. Not with armies and swords, but with the darkness that's creeping in." Silver looked around the woods. "It's speeding up now, I think. The kingdom needs old soldiers like me now more than ever."

Silver squeezed Cinder's hands before letting go.

"Go child. Be free. And may you live happily ever after."

Cinder, stunned, watched Silver as she gathered her weapons and walked away.

"Silver…"

The silver-haired woman raised her hand in farewell and continued on her way.

$\mathcal{C}$inder and the prince of Midnight followed the troll deep into the woods as the sun rose. And that was how Cinder and Dante finally became free of the dark kingdom.

Some say the troll misled them and took them to the land of fairy. The story goes that after many trials and adventures, they became the rulers of that fantastic land.

Others say the troll had told the truth and truly did lead the couple to Everness, the land of sunshine and happiness. The royal family of Everness welcomed them as permanent guests in their castle, and they became the best of friends.

Regardless of which tale people believed, no one doubted that Cinder and her prince lived happily ever after. How could they not? Anything compared to the dark kingdom must be happily ever after. That was especially true once the black shadow crept over the kingdom after the fairy became the queen.

They say that to this day, King Gallant searches for the true lady he was meant to marry. That he's convinced she was stolen by his brother into the land of fairy. He can be seen wandering through the woods, far away from his frightful queen and even more frightening children.

They say that every full moon, King Gallant can be heard in the forest, calling out for his beautiful girl with the glass slipper.

~

BOOKS BY SUSAN EE

Midnight Tales novels - fairy tales, Susan EE style:

Cinder & the Prince of Midnight

Penryn & the End of Days series - world-wide bestselling series.
Post-apocalyptic adventure with angels and fallen:

Angelfall (book 1)

World After (book 2)

End of Days (book 3)

Don't miss a new story from Susan EE!

Sign up to hear about her stories at:

www.SusanEE.com